Baz

CAOS MC

WALL STREET JOURNAL & USA TODAY
BESTSELLING AUTHOR
KB WINTERS

Copyright and Disclaimer

This book is a work of fiction. The names, characters, places and incidents are products of the writer's imagination and have been used fictitiously and are not to be construed as real. Any resemblance to persons, living or dead, actual events, locales or organizations is entirely coincidental.

Copyright © 2017 Book Boyfriends Publishing

All rights reserved. No part of this publication may be reproduced, stored in or introduced into a retrieval system, or transmitted, in any form, or by any means (electronic, mechanical, photocopying, recording, or otherwise) without the prior written permission of the copyright owner. The author acknowledges the trademarked status and trademark owners of various products referenced in this work of fiction, which have been used without permission. The publication/use of the trademarks is not authorized, associated with, or sponsored by the trademark owners.

Table of Contents

Copyright and Disclaimer ii

Prologue 5

Chapter One 17

Chapter Two 27

Chapter Three 41

Chapter Four 61

Chapter Five 78

Chapter Six 97

Chapter Seven 120

Chapter Eight 137

Chapter Nine 143

Chapter Ten 154

Epilogue 161

BAZ

CAOS MC Book 5

By KB Winters

Prologue

Trina ~ 11 years ago

"Shit yeah, baby, right there. Just like that." Damn this dream felt so real I was pretty sure I was gonna come in my sleep and I knew it was a dream because I didn't talk dirty this easily. I mean, hell, I loved sex, loved fucking, as much as any girl. And when it came to getting naked with my boyfriend Baz, my body couldn't seem to get enough. The feel of his tongue, wet and hot, against my pussy had me trembling. My pussy flooded, clenched as it swelled under his movements. His hair tangled between my fingers, soft and long. "Suck my clit," I ordered, screaming in pleasure when dream Baz obeyed. That's how I knew it was a dream. Baz, in real life, was a big fucking alpha dog. He gave me what I wanted, but never when I wanted it. His goal in the bedroom? Make me lose my fucking mind over and over again before I could even get a taste of his cock.

"Play with your tits," a deep gravelly voice commanded, instantly turning them into hard peaks, growing harder as I tugged.

"Fuck, babe. You're so good."

"Look at me Trina."

My eyes opened at the command which was a little disorienting since I'd been seeing it all so clearly. And, yep, there were those smoldering green eyes that had pulled me in when we met at a bar almost two years ago. His shaggy blonde hair in a disheveled state thanks to my greedy fingers. He smiled, my juices making his mouth and chin shiny. "Fuck. You're real."

"Damn straight, babe. I thought you were gonna wait up for me."

I smiled and rolled my hips, groaning when his lips brushed against mine. "I thought you would come home earlier." We'd started living together just six months into our relationship and I didn't keep tabs on him so when he hadn't made it home by eleven, I went to bed because I had the early morning staff meeting at a diner in town, Black Betty. We had a new owner and he wanted to meet everybody. "But this is a nice way to wake up."

"How about this," he asked and flattened his tongue, licking me from my opening to my clit before wrapping his lips around my clit and sucking hard, just how I liked it.

"Fuck yeah babe, just like that. Suck it," I said as I ground against his face, adding more pressure to my clit. Then he shoved a finger deep inside me and I felt my pussy convulse around him, squeezing him tight.

"Come for me Trina. All over me." He licked and sucked my clit, a delicious torture that started my orgasm at my toes, working its way up as his fingers speared me, hard and fast. His growl vibrated my whole body and my orgasm came.

Suddenly and with earth shattering brilliance I fell apart, my body convulsing violently while his mouth and hands slowed but didn't stop until I was safely on solid ground. And just as soon as it ended I needed more. "I want your cock Baz. Now."

"All you had to do was ask. I'm so fucking hard baby, I'm gonna pound that sweet pussy into next week."

"Promises, promises," I teased, knowing Baz loving nothing more than a challenge. Propped up on my elbows so I could watch him undress, revealing a wide, muscular body covered in tattoos. His body was a masterpiece and right now, the heated look in his eyes and the way he tugged his long hard cock, made me want to explore it with my tongue. I reached for him and he stepped back, smiling at my whimper.

"You can taste my cock later, right now all I want is to bury myself deep inside you and make you scream my name. Got it?"

Hell yeah, I got it. With a nod I summoned him forward, my eyes glued to his cock until it sank inside me, filling me up until I didn't know where he began and I ended. I loved this man and I loved the way he couldn't seem to get enough of me. He was bigger than I'd ever had, all the way around, and the things he did to my body should be illegal.

Soon he had me moaning nothing but incoherent noises because my brain had only one mission, send pleasure signals to my body. I couldn't think. Couldn't form words as he pounded into me, at first long slow strokes that teased. Then faster strokes that lit my whole fucking body on fire. "Baz," I moaned.

He smiled and gripped me behind my knee, pushing me wide open and sliding deeper, hitting that spot that meant I would be changing the sheets before we fell asleep. "Touch your clit," he commanded, eyes following my hand down between my breasts, down my belly to circle the swollen nub.

"Shit, Baz I'm gonna come."

"Yeah you are, all over my cock. Let go Trina," he pulled all the way out and thrust deep. Hard. "Now."

I flew apart, a million pieces of my heart, my body and my soul scattered around the room. Centuries from now they would find pieces of me mixed in with the cheap paint job. "Fuck. Shit."

Baz found his own release, growling my name as I milked him, still squeezing around him as his come filled me up. "Yeah I know. Love you too, babe."

He kissed me for a long time, slow sensual strokes as the mess built between us. Switching our positions so I was on top, he gripped my ass while we made out like teenagers until he slipped out of my body and we both drifted off to sleep, bodies still intertwined.

***

I slept like the dead, at least most of the night minus another round, quick, hard and intense. It felt good and when I woke up the next morning I felt good. Satisfied and relaxed. Baz still slept deeply so I grabbed a quick shower, threw on my robe and went to make breakfast. After all the calories we burned through last night, I figured we both needed to refuel and that meant chicken sausage links, French toast, eggs and fruit.

Baz was a big man with a big appetite and nothing got him hotter than his woman feeding him. I had my own selfish reasons for this big meal but I didn't have confirmation yet so I wanted to get a feel for the future of...well, us. He'd never said anything about marriage though I knew he loved me. But if this was more than simply stress, I needed to know where we stood.

"Damn, it smells good in here." His loud voice filled the quiet kitchen and I turned with a smile.

"Thanks. There's breakfast too."

"It all smells good," he said, burying his face in my long strawberry blonde hair before kissing my neck. "Good morning."

"Good morning Baz. Sleep well?"

"Would've been better if you'd been in my arms when I woke up."

Damn I couldn't resist when my big bad man got all soft and sweet. "Let's eat." We sat down and dug in while I worked up the courage to say what I needed to say. "What's next for us Baz?"

He frowned and chewed his eggs. "What do you mean next?"

"Me and you. Are we going to date indefinitely or do you want to get married someday, maybe have some kids?" Shit this was clumsy and I felt like I was pressuring him when I didn't mean to.

"Eventually I want to get married and have a few ankle biters. But not today."

Okay so that wasn't a no. But I knew eventually could mean in fifteen years which meant it wouldn't likely be with me.

"In fact, I have some news to share," he said and hopped up, taking long strides to the bedroom and back. I felt a kick in my stomach that I didn't like and when he held up the leather vest, I knew.

"What the hell is that?"

He grinned, seemingly oblivious to my distress. "My cut. I'm a prospect for the California Outlaw Specialist. CAOS."

I couldn't breathe. Couldn't think. My heart beat so fast I couldn't hear his words though I saw his lips moving. Then I felt it, bile rising in my throat. "You...what?"

His smile faded like I was the asshole raining on *his* parade. "You heard me Trina."

"But I thought we talked about this Baz." CAOS was a biker gang. Sure, they called themselves a motorcycle club but other than tinkering with bikes, they worked the wrong side of the law.

His expression morphed into a dark scowl. "No. You thought your word on my life was final. Well it ain't, sweetheart."

I couldn't believe it, shaking my head as a wave of disappointment crushed me. "You said we'd talk about it again." But obviously his word meant nothing. After two years together he'd gone and made this huge decision without me. Enough said. "Congratulations," I told him and slid between him and the wall, making my way to the bedroom. The one I was pretty sure we wouldn't be sharing for much longer.

"What's the big fucking deal Trina?"

Unbelievable! I kept my back to him because I just couldn't stand to look at him and see his anger. "The big fucking deal Baz, is that I love you. I am so in love with you that all I can think about is the life we *could* have. But when I see you in that vest with that patch, all I can see is pain and heartache and danger. I see my dad lying dead in the driveway because he owed the wrong person money he couldn't pay back."

When I closed my eyes, I could still see Dad lying there in the driveway beside our shitty two-tone blue escort with two holes in his chest and lifeless eyes staring up at me. Only this time it wasn't Dad, it was Baz. And like the wimp I was, I cried and cried, shaking off his attempt to soothe me. "I can't go through that again Baz."

"Baby, I've survived way worse than what CAOS can offer up and I'll survive this too." He moved again to wrap me in his arms but I pushed him away because I knew the comfort he provided would have me caving in no time.

"I love you Baz, more than you know. But I can't live through that again. I'm sorry."

He let out a long sigh. When he spoke again, his voice was annoyed but I still didn't look up at him. "This is happening Trina, get used to it," he said. The sound of his heavy boots walking away told me he'd given up on this conversation. "We'll talk more when you calm down." The only sound that came next was the door slamming behind him.

I spent two days waiting for him to come home and he never did. That's when I knew we couldn't work it out. He was probably over at the compound fucking some random girl looking to become a biker babe, someone who would lie down to his way of life. And if my late period turned out to be more than stress, I knew I couldn't live that kind of life.

I packed up my clothes, my pillow and a few kitchen essentials I'd need no matter where I landed. When noon came and went on the third day I got the message loud and clear. With all my worldly possessions loaded up in my six-year-old Camry, I slid behind the wheel, wiped away my tears and began to drive.

I never imagined I'd have to start over again, especially without Baz. Now I could only hope I wouldn't end up like my dad, all alone and completely unequipped to raise a child.

Chapter One

Baz

Days like this I wished I still smoked. Nothing like sucking back a Camel to make shit like wedding menus a little less annoying. What the fuck did I know about weddings, anyway? Not one goddamn thing, that's what. There had been a time—a long fucking time ago—that I thought about marriage. Hell, that there was a woman I'd actually wanted to spend forever with but she up and left without notice. That's when I knew guys like me weren't cut out for happy endings and forever, or any of that lovey dovey shit.

But Torch was my friend. My fellow brother in arms. Hell, he'd taken care of my kid sister Cherie when I was off fighting on behalf of corrupt politicians and the corporations who paid for them. So yeah, I owed him. And apparently wedding menus were how he wanted me to repay the debt. There was no use bitching about it any longer and since I didn't have a smoke, I went inside Black Betty where I knew pretty much everyone.

"Want some coffee Baz?" Talon flashed a smile, her belly growing with her second child. She and Mick were the happiest parents I'd ever seen.

"Sure thing. And some of that chicken fried steak on special today," I told her and took a seat in the middle of the counter. This time of day the place didn't have any customers but a few old guys sat to my left and a kid played on my right. "How's that baby treatin' ya?"

She smiled bright, rubbing her belly. "Great, thanks. I'll be right back."

Talon was a good woman and a great fit for the club president, Mick. Though she'd come to Brently to claim her inheritance, she'd fallen for the man her father had treated like a son. *She* had an open mind when it came to the club and CAOS business. Unlike some other people. *Where the fuck did that thought come from?* I had no clue but I needed to get my shit together. It wouldn't do me any good to start reliving the past.

"Hey Baz."

"Hey Kyla, where's your grumpy groom to be?"

She grinned and took a seat beside me. "He dropped me off in front and then went to park. Apparently, everyone is out and about today."

The Founder's Day parade would be held in about a week which meant committees were out decorating and setting up for the big event. A bandstand was being built in the park and soon the main drag would be filled with booths selling food, crafts, booze and other wares. "You forget what small-town living is like already?"

She laughed. "No but I kind of took it all for granted back then. It's nice now though, knowing my kid will have the same kind of upbringing."

"Yeah good for you guys." I was happy for Torch, the same way I was happy for Mick and Cash and even our old prez, Roddick. They'd all found nice girls, women too damn good for them, and settled down.

19

They were doing the whole wife and kids thing. I envied them, but I felt like I'd pissed away my chance at that life. "So, what are we doing here?"

"The table in the back is occupied so we wait."

"Or we take another table?"

Kyla smacked her bag. "No can do. We need the space."

I was about to tell her to spread that shit out right here so we could get it over and done but something cracked my fucking elbow. "Shit!" Rubbing my funny bone, I turned ready to rip someone a new asshole, only it wasn't just a someone. It was a kid with the biggest green eyes I'd ever seen.

"Sorry mister, it was an accident," the little boy said as he shrank away from me.

That pissed me off. Clearly there was a man in this boy's life who frightened him and I didn't put up with anyone who beat women or kids. If that asshole was here I'd fuck him up. For the kid, I smiled and ruffled his hair. "Don't worry about it little man, shit happens."

He gasped. "You said a bad word."

Shit, I had. "I'm a grownup so it's okay."

He grinned. "Okay. I'm Jack, what's your name."

"My friends call me Baz. Want to tell me what's wrong with your car?"

He lifted up a shiny new remote-controlled race car. "The dang thing don't drive right."

That was a problem I could fix. "That's easy. You just need a light touch. You ever played a video game before?"

"Uh-huh. Lots. But Mom doesn't let me play the really cool ones."

Which meant the violent ones. "Okay well what happens if you move the controller too hard?"

"It messes up."

"Exactly. Same here. You just need a light touch," I took the remote and showed him, sending the car straight to the end of the counter, busting out a three-point turn and coming right back. "Now you try it."

21

He did it without a problem and whooped loud, holding his little hand up for a high five. "I did it, mister! I did it! Thanks."

"No problem kid." Shit had I ever been that young? So trusting and carefree? "How old are you kid?"

"Ten. How old are you?"

I laughed at that. "Much older than ten. Where are your parents?"

"Mom's back there getting some work done. I don't know my dad though."

Damn. Tough break.

"Hey Baz, you comin'?"

Torch called from the back and I hadn't even noticed him enter. I nodded and turned to the kid. "I need to go help my friends, Jack. Take it easy kid."

"Okay," he sounded a little sad to see me go. "Thank you, Mr. Baz. Bye."

Mr. Baz. No one ever addressed me so formally and I couldn't help but smile. It'd been a long time since I spent any time with kids but that Jack was a good kid. Lost in my thoughts as I made my way to the big table in the back of Black Betty where Minx was huddled close to a head of shoulder-length strawberry blonde hair. "Hey Minx, what's up?"

She looked up and smiled, glowing with the happiness of yet another pregnancy. I swear all these guys did was fuck. "Baz you devil, how's it going? You here to help with the menus?"

"Yep. Torch guilted me into it, you?"

"I'm finishing up a job with a new client, this is-,"

"Trina?" I said the moment she turned and faced me. I'd never forget that face, beautiful and fresh with a sprinkling of freckles. I hadn't seen her in more than a fucking decade after she'd skipped out on me.

"Baz," she replied icily. She wasn't happy to see me, that was for goddamn sure, but the question I wanted to know was why. She'd been the one who left. "If you'll excuse us, we have some work to finish here."

Dismissed. But not quite. "Actually, my friends have reserved this table so I believe your work here is finished."

"Damn, Baz," Minx chided, "don't be an asshole."

"He can't help it," Trina said, packing up her laptop and a bunch of papers. "It's his way or no way at all. Thanks for your help Minx. Let me know a good time to go over the rest and just send me your bill." She hoisted the big patchwork bag on her shoulder and handed Minx a couple books.

"Oh my goodness, thank you!" She pulled Trina into a hug. "I can't believe you're *you*. Wait until I tell Talon and Trudy, they're going to shit a brick!" She squealed and—amazingly—Trina blushed. "We'll get together again soon and you can meet some of the girls."

Trina pulled a card from her pocket and scribbled on the back. "That's my cell. Give me a call whenever and thank you, for everything."

I watched her walk away with the same swing in her hips that had pulled me in twelve, or was it thirteen years ago when I'd seen her in that bar. Her hair was shorter now but she still smelled like fresh peaches and sunshine. Her legs were still long and lean under that denim skirt, and had more muscle than when we were younger. A pink blouse hid most of her figure but I could still make out the shape of those spectacular tits. Shaped just like teardrops.

"Okay, dude. I know there's a story there and I want it," Minx whispered with a little too much glee for my liking.

I grunted at Minx but I couldn't take my eyes off Trina, heart stopping as she paused in front of Jack, who wrapped his hand around hers before they made their way to the door. He turned, pointed at me and said something to her before waving and Trina froze, quickly herding Jack out the door. Shit. Jack was *her* son? Trina was a mom. Probably had a husband too. Every fucking thing she ever wanted.

"I see you made quite the impression on Jack," Minx said, amusement in her voice.

"Where's the husband," I asked finally turning to Minx even though the truth was I couldn't give a fuck. Mostly.

"Husband? She never married."

The last thing I wanted to hear and also the best fucking news I heard all day. "Fucking wedding menus," I grumbled and took the seat Trina had just vacated.

Chapter Two

Trina

Baz was still in Brently. Hell, it was more of a shock he hadn't died or ended up in prison over the past decade. But he looked more than alive. He looked hotter than ten types of sin and even I could admit he wore the sexy outlaw biker look like a second skin. If I hadn't already known it, I would shake my fists at the universe about the unfairness of it all. Why couldn't Baz have gone bald or gotten fat? Why was he still so damn sexy?

I knew I should have prepared myself for the possibility of seeing him again. Maybe I subconsciously wanted to see him?

Coming back to Brently made it very likely, and I guessed I'd done a good job of pushing any good thoughts of him far from my mind over the years. I could conjure up what an asshole he'd been in two seconds flat.

Two weeks after leaving Brently, I took a pregnancy test to confirm what I already knew when I pushed my Camry east, and far away from the man who broke my heart. I'd found a Planned Parenthood and got a blood test and I knew I'd made the right decision to leave. But now, seeing him and still being affected as though I was still a twenty-year-old girl, completely in love with him, I had to wonder.

No. I didn't. With Baz's lifestyle, Jack and I would always be at risk for whatever shit the club had gotten into. He didn't know anything about Jack and for the time being, I wanted to keep it that way.

"Hey Mom did you see? That man with the tattoos on his body? I want one!"

They didn't even know each other, neither knew about the other but already Baz had made an impression on my—*our*—son. "When you turn eighteen you can decide for yourself. But remember you'll have to find a job to buy all the things your mean old mom won't get for you."

He laughed and as always, I was struck with how much he already resembled Baz. I could only hope he didn't notice it too. "I'll bet Mr. Baz has a job!"

Yeah, riding motorcycles and kicking up trouble, no doubt. "Well lucky for him I'm not his mother." Thank fuck for that because I felt a lot of things towards Baz—love, hate, lust and even resentment—but not maternal. And now that I'd laid eyes on him, I regretted choosing Brently as my refuge even though I had my reasons and those reasons meant I needed to make sure Jack and I were safe. Specifically, one very bad reason and he would soon be released from prison.

"He was nice to me Mom even though I hit him with my car!"

And I knew how much that meant to my son. My ex, Jensen, had been nothing but dismissive of Jack from the moment they met. He was never mean or abusive but he pretended Jack didn't exist. The first two times I thought it might just be the case of him trying to get used to being around a kid but by the fifth time it became clear he wanted me without a kid.

Which meant he had to go. We'd had six good months before I let him meet my son and a month after we were done. Seven months of dating and the man had pretty much stalked me for next three years. If not for the fact the Feds caught him embezzling and trading illegally, he'd still be going strong.

But Jensen was in a white-collar prison, a country club, and he'd be up for parole soon which meant he thought we'd pick up where we left off. So like the strong, fierce, independent woman I was, I ran as fast as I could to the other side of the country. Home. Brently.

And smack into an entirely different problem. A six foot three, sexy green-eyed problem.

By the time I pulled into the driveway of our little ranch house with the blue and yellow shutters I didn't feel much better about, hell anything. This would be our home for the foreseeable future with three bedrooms, it was perfect for us. A bedroom for each of us and an office for me. With no living family, there was no need for a guest room and I didn't anticipate having more children so we had more than enough room. Though I imagined when Jack began to make friends, sleepovers would make the place feel a lot smaller.

"Can I play outside Mom?"

"Sure. Just stay on this block sweetie. I'll be in my office for a while." My office, where I'd created the means to take care of my baby. When I first learned I was pregnant I worked twelve-hour shifts as a waitress and although I made good money, I knew it couldn't be my future. So, I wrote a romance novel and got rejected by pretty much everyone.

Unwilling to let it go after I found a passion for it, I decided to self-publish under a penname. And while I waited for my millions to roll in, I put my own life on a budget and created *Mommy's Little Budget*. It had been a constant struggle, finding ways to put money in the bank for bills, diapers and rent but then right around Jack's fifth birthday it all sort of came together. An agent signed me and got me a book deal within six months and then she got my blog syndicated and sponsored which meant I didn't have to buy a lot of necessities any longer. Jack had all the things a little boy could want or need, including a parent there for everything. We had a home of our own, we went on family vacations and weekend road trips. It was perfect.

Until Jensen.

Jensen—along with my desire to start dating again—had fucked it all up. He made my home feel like a prison. Made me afraid to answer my own phone. Leaving was the best thing for us both. Even if it meant seeing Baz regularly.

"Mom!" Jack let the door smack shut behind him, his growing feet smacking clumsily on the wood floors. "The man from the restaurant, Mr. Baz, is here. To see you!" Big green eyes gleamed and I had a feeling Jack was trying to play matchmaker.

Baz. The last person I expected on my doorstep. "I'll be right there Jack." So much for getting more work done. I'd already been at it over an hour, and I'd barely gotten two thousand words on my latest novel, *Sins of the Hourglass*, completed. That's what nights were for, I reminded myself as I wiped nervous hands on my skirt and took a deep, cleansing breath.

Now I was ready. To face my past. And there he was, sitting on my front porch like he belonged there, watching Jack perfect his skateboard tricks. "Baz. What are you doing here?"

Slowly he pulled his gaze from Jack and set those unforgettable emerald green eyes on me. And grinned. "I came to see you, Sweetness."

Sweetness. God, I hadn't heard that name in forever. He'd always called me that and I loved it, felt treasured because of it. What a lie it had been. "What do you want?"

"Cool kid," he said instead of answering my question.

Yeah he was. "He's the best. Now tell me what you want or leave." I kept my expression and my tone neutral so Jack didn't feel alarmed. Or threatened.

His gaze never left Jack and that's when I felt it, that uneasy feeling I'd had when the Connecticut D.A.

called to tell me Jensen would be up for parole in six months. That had been three months ago. I heeded it then but now it seemed to be too late. He watched Jack flip the board in a full rotation under his feet. "We have some things to talk about, don't you think sweetness?"

"Oh yeah? Like what?" I didn't think it would work but I hoped Baz was just fishing. He couldn't have put it all together so quickly and even if he did, denial was my best friend.

He looked over his shoulder, blonde brows high in an expression that said it all. *Really?*

I sighed and rolled my eyes. "Maybe we do but I don't see what we'd possibly have to talk about. Even if we did—but we don't—now is definitely not the time." Not with Jack close enough to hear it all. "I'll see you around Baz." I had no desire to rehash that old fight, which I knew he was itching to do. I didn't have time either, I had a book to finish and a blog to update.

This new life was mine and no one, not even Baz would derail it.

***

"You have a collect call from Osborn Correctional Facility from Jensen Murray, do you wish to accept the call?" The robotic voice sounded so benign, couldn't possibly know how much fear she'd brought into my home.

"Hell no!" I hung up the phone, pulse pounding as I struggled to breathe. That call meant one damn thing. Jensen had found me. Jack and I had been back in Brently for a couple weeks and already Jensen had our location and number. *Fuck my life.*

"Mornin' Mom! Can we have hash browns today? You make 'em the best!"

How could I look at that adorable face, peppered with freckles and resist? I couldn't. I sautéed up some onions and bell peppers while I grated a couple of potatoes, listening to Jack tell me all about the book he'd just finished. "Breakfast will be ready when the bacon is done, better go and get dressed kiddo." It was something I had to be careful with, working from home. I wanted Jack up and dressed for the day at a decent hour.

"Aww, Mom, do I have to?" But he scrambled off anyway because though apparently my boy hated taking showers, I knew he was excited about the day ahead. When he came back with damp hair all over the place, he grinned and poured himself a glass of milk. "What are we doing?"

"Eat up and I'll tell you on the way." He gave a quick pout but much like his father, he couldn't resist the taste of apple smoked bacon. We ate mostly in silence, Jack trying to figure out what we were doing today and me trying to figure out if I should pack up and leave again or just change my number.

By the time we reached the community center I hadn't made any decision other than finding something to keep my boy busy during the summer. And maybe make some friends. "I'd like you to be part of the reading club, keep your skills up. If you take it then you can choose something else." Provided it didn't cost too much and wouldn't kill him.

His grin spread wide, slightly cocky just like another green-eyed devil I knew. Or used to know. "You mean I could sign up for rock climbing?"

"Rock climbing? Why on earth would you want to do that?"

"Because it's cool."

I rolled my eyes. "Yes. After I've spoken with the instructor."

"Next!"

I turned and my eyes went wide. "Trudy? Trudy Jacobs, is that you?"

Her eyes flashed with recognition and a smile lit up her face reminding me of the beautiful girl with the golden eyes I'd known in high school. "Oh. My. God. Trina Mosley? Girl you look exactly the same as the day we graduated high school."

I rolled my eyes. "Yeah right. How are you?"

"Great. I'm still married but I've had another kid since you left town. My youngest will be twelve this year," she said as her gaze slid to Jack who looked up at her with fascination. "And who is this handsome young man?"

"I'm Jack," he said and offered up his hand, making me so proud.

"I'm Trudy and it's nice to meet you Jack. How old are you?"

"Ten. How old are you?"

"Jack!" Why would he ask that?

"I'm just being polite Mom, asking about her."

Trudy only laughed and dropped a hand on his shoulder, we'd become friends when she tutored me in freshman algebra so I knew she was running some quick calculations in her head. "I'm old enough that my youngest kid is older than you." Trudy went back around the counter and looked at me. "I guess you're here for summer activities?"

I let her and Jack go back and forth on activities because seeing Trudy, well it all just kind of came back to me. We'd been friends in school and spent time together when Baz started showing more interest in the gang.

"Mom are you listening?"

"No, but I am now. Tell me."

He rolled his eyes as only a child could and repeated himself. "Reading club, rock climbing and kid mechanics."

I slid a glance at Trudy who just smiled innocently. "Fine," I told Jack because I didn't want to explain to him why it might be a problem.

"I'm gonna learn how to fix cars Mom, isn't that cool?"

Cool wasn't the word I'd use but as we made our way to one of the classrooms I felt slightly nauseous. A tad apprehensive. "So cool," I deadpanned as the door opened to reveal Baz leaning on the hood of a partially disassembled car.

"Mr. Baz are you in this class too?"

"Nah, I'm standing in for a buddy. Today I'm the teacher." He flashed a bright wide smile, eyes full of mischief.

"Cool! Mom it's Mr. Baz!"

And it was too late to do anything other than paste a damn smile on my face because I'd already handed Trudy my bank card and agreed to it all. "Yep." Jack needed a chance to have some masculine influence in his life and interact with other kids his age, and this would be perfect. This, along with his other classes would help him make friends before school started in the fall which I guessed meant I was staying in Brently.

Because my life wasn't fucking complicated enough.

Chapter Three

Baz

"Hey man, what's up?" Cash strolled into the empty classroom wearing a big ass grin that said he'd woken up and loved his wife good and proper.

"Got a lot on my mind." I was so focused on the new engine I didn't even hear the fucker creep up on me. This shit with Trina had me all twisted up and though I had my suspicions, her denial pissed me off.

"Want to talk about it?"

"Are we gonna eat bon bons too and share a box of Kleenex?" I grinned over my shoulder and he punched my arm. "What the hell, man?"

"You obviously want to talk Baz, so stop being a fuckhead and tell me what it is so I can help."

"You think you can help me?" I didn't think anyone could help me and especially not a boy scout type like Cash.

"Won't know until I hear it. Now stop bullshitting and just tell me what's up."

What the hell did I have to lose, right? Cash didn't know shit of my history with her so I had to tell the whole damn story. Which I did. "There was a girl and we were good together. Like you and Minx good. But it was before CAOS and she didn't approve when I got my cut, so she left. Now she's back and she has a ten-year-old kid. And she'd left me eleven years ago. That leaves two options."

"You're worried she had your kid and didn't tell you."

"Yep." I nodded, clenching my fists tight so I wouldn't ruin any of the donated car parts.

"Or worse, the kid isn't yours and she fell into someone else's bed shortly after leaving town?"

"Fuck!"

"You could just ask her. It has been known to produce answers ya know."

"You don't think I fucking asked? She gave me a non-denial denial." Which made me think she was hiding my son from me but the Trina I knew would never do that. She'd also never hop into bed with a stranger.

"Why would she lie? She had to know you'd still be in town."

"That's what I thought too. She said she didn't think I was even alive anymore."

"Shit." His brows arched in surprise and Cash gave a sympathetic shake of his head. "She probably didn't tell you because she didn't think you were still around." It wasn't a question. "But now?"

"Now," I sighed, "I need to know. The kid looks a lot like me but I'm fucking going out of my mind. Is he mine, or isn't he? Why do I even give a fuck? Obviously, she doesn't want me involved, doesn't think I'm father material, so does it even matter? Do I even wanna do that to a kid? Get him all fucked up over who's his daddy?"

"Wow." Cash leaned back on the desk, legs crossed at the ankle with a smug fucking look on his face.

"What?"

"I knew you got a lot of pussy Baz, but I didn't think you were one."

I froze and glared at him. "Careful motherfucker. I can still kick your ass." I was itching for a fight and Cash's pretty little face would be the perfect punching bag.

And then the bastard chuckled. "I'll give you one punch because honestly, a long-lost kid is some big shit, but then I'd have to pound your skanky ass into the ground old man. Minx likes my face just the way it is." He batted his eyelashes like a broad and goddammit I laughed.

"You are one crazy son of a bitch."

His smile stayed in place but those pretty boy eyes were deadly serious. "Give me an hour and her social and I'll see whose name is on the kid's birth certificate."

"I don't have it, but she's staying in Cherie's old place and she ended up in Connecticut. I have no fucking clue where she was when she had him." If he was mine, that was just one more goddamn thing I didn't know.

"Chill. I'll get back with you at the end of the day."

I gave a short nod. "Fine. Let's get ready for the kiddies then. You can meet Jack."

***

Trina was avoiding me and I had a feeling that the little blonde headed boy with the big green eyes who hadn't left my side in two weeks was why. Jack though, was great. He had a shit ton of energy, asked plenty of good questions and quickly picked up the basics of auto mechanics. His hunger for male attention just confirmed that he hadn't enough of it in his short life. The boy had to be mine no matter what Trina wanted me to believe. And now that Cash was looking into it for me, we could finally have that talk.

Cash had taken over the class, but I decided to stick around anyway because I wanted to ambush Trina before she could whisk Jack away. The little guy would be my ally even if he didn't know it just yet. Waiting outside the community center, twenty minutes had come and gone and still Trina hadn't shown up. "Where do you think your mom is?"

Jack shrugged. "She probably got lost in her work. She'll be really sorry when she remembers." His words were so matter of fact it kind of threw me.

"You don't mind?"

"Nah. Mom's great and usually when she gets like this I end up staying up late or watchin' something I'm not supposed to." His mischievous grin reminded me so much of my kid sister for a moment I had to take a step back.

My kid. Shit that was a huge responsibility and I wasn't sure, even now, if I was ready for it. "Come on then, I'll give you a ride home."

Jack grinned when I set my helmet on his head, laughing when I picked him up and set him on the back of the bike. "I'm not gonna go fast but I still want you to hang on tight, all right?"

He frowned. "You're not gonna go fast?"

"Nah. Your mom would kick my ass." She might try, anyway.

He laughed. "She would yell at you until you wanted to cry but she wouldn't hurt you. Mom says violence isn't the answer unless you're defending yourself."

I bit back a response to that and hopped on, starting the engine and then we were off. I took the shortest route to the same house where my sister Cherie used to live before moving to Canada with the former CAOS president, Roddick.

It was fucking surreal. Coming here after the place sat empty for so long, now though it was kind of ironic that my past came back to this house. I cut the engine and helped Jack down. The kid had so much energy, bounding up the steps and pulling me inside.

"Mom! Mom! You forgot me again." His voice carried through the silent house and I wondered if Trina was even there. But Jack stopped outside the door and knocked. "This is her office. I'm not allowed in here except for emergencies." But I could tell the kid was impatient from his tapping foot to his huffing breath and he knocked again. "Mom!"

She pulled the door open with a sleepy-eyed frown. "Did class finish early?"

"Nope. You zoned out. Again."

And just like that, tears welled in her eyes and she dropped down and wrapped the boy in a tight hug. "Oh God, sweetie I'm so sorry. Zelda called earlier and started making some changes to the story and I got wrapped up. Forgive me?" She smiled but it was uncertain.

It was clear to me Jack had been the man of the house for a long time as he touched Trina's face. "Of course, Mom. No big deal."

Then her gaze turned to me. "Thank you, Baz."

"No problem, Sweetness."

With his free hand, Jack grabbed mine. It was so damned tiny; how did kids ever survive this small? "Can Baz stay for dinner?"

Damn! I loved this kid. I didn't even have to con my way into an invitation. Trina stared, preparing to say no and I lifted my brows in defiance. The rejection was poised on those lush lips of hers but suddenly she softened, her body relaxed as she nodded. "Baz would you like to join us for dinner?"

"Sure thing, Sweetness. Sounds fun."

"It is," Jack insisted excitedly, jumping up and down. "Mom is the best cook and I'm gonna be even better, won't I?"

Trina nodded and gave him an indulgent smile. "I sure hope so then these old bones can let you do all the cooking," she ruffled his hair. "How does lasagna sound?"

Jack gasped. "Oh Baz you are so lucky. I love lasagna!"

Seeing Trina as a mother was a trip. I still wanted to see her as the young girl who'd been head over heels for me but she was older. Wiser. A mother through and through. I couldn't shake the anger in me that Jack had been without me all these years, but now wasn't the time to deal with that. Later we would have a chance to talk. I would make sure of it. "What do you need me to do," I asked when we all stepped inside the kitchen.

Trina stood still for just a moment, back facing me and Jack then she turned and began to move. "Jack, you shred the cheddars and Baz you can break up the tomatoes," she ordered and set us both up on the table with everything we needed. "I'll chop and sauté the onions, peppers and meat. Got it?"

"Got it," Jack shouted back.

"Got it sweetness."

Jack frowned. "Why do you call her that?"

"I used to know your mom a long time ago and that's what I called her. Because she was so sweet."

Jack laughed, picking up fingers of shredded cheese and sneaking it into his mouth. "Sweetness."

Damn it kind of hurt to watch them like this. They joked and worked together like a team that had been together for a while. It pissed me off but fuck it also made me feel warm inside. I just wanted to know why.

Thirty minutes later the lasagna was assembled and in the oven and we had time to kill. It was the perfect time to talk. Then the phone rang and Trina stiffened, distress written all over her face. Her posture. She bypassed the phone in the kitchen and ducked into the living room.

Jack rolled his eyes with a groan. "I'll bet that's Jensen. Again."

A boyfriend? More importantly one Jack didn't like, was interesting. And unlike Trina. "Who's Jensen?"

Jack sighed and his shoulders slumped. "Mom dated him for a while but he didn't like me all that much so she got rid of him but he won't stop calling or showing up. He's in jail for stealing from his company, but he still calls." He leaned towards me, gaze on the doorway so I knew what he had to say would be juicy. "We moved away because he's getting out soon but I think that's him again."

Shit. I wanted to ask another question. Hell, another fifty questions but the phone slammed down and soon Trina walked back in stiffly with a too bright smile slapped on. "Okay who's ready for salad?"

"Make the dressing creamy and we have a deal," I told her, enjoying the grateful smile she sent my way. Damn the woman could still knock me on my ass with a look. Big blue eyes as deep as the Pacific with a smattering of freckles on the bridge of her nose that gave her a deceptive innocence.

She frowned. "No can do. Only healthy homemade vinaigrette in this house." She pointed at

Jack when he groaned, drawing a smile from him. "It'll be delicious or you can eat your salad dry."

"Don't do it," Jack whispered with a grave expression on his face.

I could only laugh. Otherwise I might yell at Trina for all she'd deprived me of by leaving. By not bothering to inform me she was having my baby. "Fine. Vinaigrette it is."

She flashed a smile and set a big wooden bowl in the center of the table while Jack grabbed bowls and silverware. "Dig in boys."

Shit this was nice. A family dinner. The last time I'd sat down for one of those, I wasn't much older than Jack and damnit! I missed it. Even with just a few people there were several conversations going on at once about Jack's classes, a planned trip to Arizona and school shopping. How they kept track of them amazed me. Left me envious and I fucking hated pointless emotions like that.

But all throughout dinner envy was the only thing I felt while they laughed and planned and walked down Memory Lane. "Baz do you have a girlfriend?"

"Why kid, you interested?"

Jack laughed and rolled his eyes, a move I was coming to associate with him. "Not like that. So, do you?"

"Not at the moment." The truth was, I never had girlfriends. I had women I fucked. The lucky ones got fucked more than once, but not too often or they started to get ideas. I didn't need or want an old lady and the *pass-arounds* were looking to get promoted to old lady. No thank you.

"Mom doesn't have a boyfriend either," he replied with a cheeky tomato sauce smile as he devoured his second piece of lasagna.

"Jack that's enough," she told him. "Baz and I knew each other long ago and that's it."

"But-,"

"No buts young man."

Wow, Trina really was. A. Fucking. Mom.

Jack huffed out his displeasure and turned to me. "Can I ask you another question Baz?"

"Sure kiddo, what is it?"

"Are you my dad?"

Well.

Fuck.

I never expected that.

***

"You have to tell him Trina." After Jack dropped his little bomb on dinner, dessert was eaten mostly in silence. Trina looked worried and Jack just looked pissed off while I simply enjoyed a slice of German chocolate cake.

"I'll tell him when I'm ready Baz and not a minute before." She walked out of the kitchen and took a seat on a plush blue sofa with a view out the front window.

"It's not about you Trina. It's about Jack. Why not tell him what all three of us already knows is true?"

"You don't know what it means to tell him Baz. Right now you're just some cool guy who's nice to him but once he knows for sure, he'll have expectations. He's never had a father before, or a father figure. He'll expect you to spend time with him, to be there for him."

"And you don't think I'll do that?"

"How in the hell should I know? I don't know you anymore."

I stood just a few feet away from her, my hands fisted on my hips and glared down at her. "But you knew me eleven years ago when you never bothered to fucking tell me you were pregnant. Or that you had my baby!"

Trina was cool as fuck. One leg crossed over the other at the knee, hands folded in her lap. "You should've thought about that before you put your needs above ours."

"You know I'm not like that."

She stood up, we were face to face and she poked at my chest. "You made this choice, Baz, not me."

I barked out an angry laugh. "Oh please. Obviously you're back here because you couldn't find someone else to play daddy to my son."

In a split second, her hand flew out and she smacked my face hard enough to sting and shocked the shit out of me. Apparently, Sweetness had grown some claws.

"I didn't come back for you Baz, trust me. I had no idea whether you were dead or alive!"

"What the fuck do you mean by that? You knew where I was. You could have told me."

"Yeah well I didn't. I loved you Baz. I wanted you, but all you wanted was your precious fucking club."

That wasn't true at all. The truth was, her leaving had ripped me wide open and after seeing her again, I wasn't sure I'd fully recovered. But right now, she wouldn't be able to hear it. "So that meant I didn't get to know my son?"

"I thought about telling you but I was busy. Earning the money I needed to take care of my son." She sighed and ran a shaky hand through her hair. "Then I called once and some woman answered and I knew it was better that you didn't know. I figured you'd be married or dead soon and there was no point in breaking my son's heart."

"What the hell does that mean?"

"It means he was better off not knowing you at all than knowing you and losing you."

"Stop saying that!" I hadn't meant to roar or get in her face but goddammit it, she was pissing me off. "I'm still here. Not married. Not dead. So you better find a way to tell Jack that he's my son."

"I will," she answered, her chin tilted defiantly. "When I'm ready. DNA doesn't give you a say here Baz and I won't let you come in and dictate things."

I grabbed her wrists and pulled her in close. "Soon," I growled, inhaling that sweet scent that was all Trina. Then I did the thing I'd been dreaming of doing since I saw her in Black Betty. Hell, since I stormed out of our apartment eleven years ago. I cupped her face in my hands and kissed her. Licking her lips until she opened them, tasting every inch of her like the hungry, greedy bastard I was.

She moaned into my mouth and I deepened the kiss, sliding my hands through her hair and down her back until they settled on her ass. Goddamn that was one fine ass. More than a handful. The perfect cushion for fucking her from behind. For smacking and leaving a red print of my hand. Fuck yeah, she felt so damn good all I wanted to do was sink my cock deep inside her.

Too damn soon she pushed me back. "I can't go there with you again Baz. I'll talk to Jack, soon, and then we can talk about what's next."

I wanted to toss her over my shoulder and lose myself in her sweet curvy body for the rest of the night. Instead I stepped back and nodded. "Then I'll see you later, Sweetness."

I kissed her again and left.

Chapter Four

Trina

Damn Baz and those panty scorching, bone melting kisses and damn me for allowing him to do it.

Days later, my mouth still tingled from his kiss, his handprint still burned on my ass. Why, after all this time, did Baz still have the power to turn me inside out? To electrify my senses? Of all the billions of men in the world, it had to be him who kept me so hot and bothered that I couldn't sleep.

The only upside to my sleeplessness was that those waking hours were spent in my office, typing until my fingers cramped and my back was stiff. I made good progress on the second half of *Sins of the Hourglass* and I was pretty confident I had the beginnings of an outline for the next book. So even after kissing me like an oaf, claiming I came back to Brently because of *him* and trying to push me to tell Jack about him, I couldn't even be mad at him.

The fucker.

What I could stay mad about was the fact the hero in my story had suddenly begun to look and act like the fair haired bad boy who'd stolen—and then broken—my heart more than a decade ago.

"Shit!" There was another thing to blame on Baz, burnt eggs. I tossed them in the garbage and started over. "Jack, it's time for breakfast!"

The sound of his growing feet smacked against the floor, until he stopped at the table and then dropped into his seat. "What are we having?"

"Eggs, bacon and toast because we have to get a move on buddy." Eventually I'd have to talk to him about Baz but I wasn't ready. Not yet.

"Fine." He piled his plate with bacon and eggs, taking just one slice of toast until I gave him *the look*. "Fine," he groaned and took another slice. The little stinker had something on his mind so I took a small bite and waited until he was ready. "I've seen the pictures of you guys Mom."

And there we were. "Pictures?"

"Of you and Baz together. Hugging and kissing and stuff. You were a couple."

I nodded because there would be no point in hiding that much. "Yes, we were." How Baz and I could be boiled down to a word as simple as couple seemed unbelievable, but that's what we were. Two people who used to know each other.

"So, he is my dad?"

I sighed. "We'll talk about this tonight at dinner, okay?"

He wasn't happy but nodded anyway. "Whatever."

I let it stand, because he wanted to know and he deserved to know the truth and I promised myself as I drove him to the community center, I'd gather up my courage and we'd have the conversation.

Tonight.

After dropping him off, I stopped to get groceries along with a few other items for my next blog post.

Days like this made me wish I had a few friends to lounge with in the yard, maybe throw some burgers and steaks on the grill. Instead, I had to work. My novel wasn't going to write itself.

I put the groceries away and headed to my office when I heard the mailman. I doubted there was any good news in there but I'd rather have bad news while Jack was away.

As usual there were tons of coupons, the local newspaper and a postcard. Fuck. From Jensen. All it said was, "See you soon," in his prissy little scrawl that made me want to break something. "Fuck! Shit! Goddamn you Jensen!" I wouldn't let that bastard ruin my new life. I would fight back.

"That's a lot of nastiness coming from such a sweet little mouth." Baz.

"What are you doing here? Shouldn't you be in class?"

Baz shook his head as he climbed the steps, putting his hand to the small of my back and pushing me inside. "Cash is back so my assistance is no longer required. Want to tell me why you were out here cursing like a biker?"

The last thing I wanted was to involve Baz in this so I slid the postcard into my back pocket and shook my head. "Nope."

His mouth curled up into an amused smile that reminded of the young man I'd fallen in love with and I felt my knees wobble. I had to lock them to stop his effect on me. "Are we seriously going to do this?" He moved in, invading my space. One hand slid up to my waist and under my shirt, the pads of his fingers slid across my ribcage, teasing me. His other hand grabbed my ass and then, "Yeah that's what I thought."

"Hey!" I reached for the postcard he'd slid from my pocket, but Baz held it out of my reach. "Fucker."

He just laughed when I pushed at him, grabbing my wrists in one hand as his gaze scanned the card. "Is this your asshole ex?" At my surprised look, he explained. "Jack told me."

Of course he did. "Yeah it's him. Somehow, he's already found out where we are. He gets out soon and thinks we'll be together." I'd left because he had nine years of parole which meant he was stuck in Connecticut for the foreseeable fucking future.

"Hey, Sweetness. You know I'm not going to let that fucker near either one of you, don't you?"

I did know and that was exactly why I didn't want Baz involved. But I nodded because now that he knew Jack was his, I wouldn't be able to keep him from interfering.

"Now," he tossed the card on the table and pulled me by the waist until our bodies were pressed so close I could feel his heartbeat. "We have some unfinished business, don't we?"

I felt his cock grow between us and all I could think about was how it would feel sliding between my thighs. Thrusting into me hard and fast, the way we almost always came together. My body was nothing more than a pool of lust and desire as he held me. My pussy clenched and my breasts hung heavy, my nipples hard and aching. I hissed out a breath when his hips pressed hard into me.

"I can't hear you Trina."

That snapped me out of my lust fueled haze. "I told you I'd talk to Jack in my own time."

"I appreciate that Trina, I really do. But," he grabbed my ass and lifted me, forcing my legs to tighten around his waist. "That's not the business I'm talking about. This is," he told me, brushing his lips against mine so softly I let out a whimper. His lips were soft and warm as they pressed their way down my neck, leaving a trail of wet heat that lit my body on fire.

I moaned. Or maybe I whimpered as his cock rocked onto me and then we were falling onto my bed and his hands slipped into the waistband of my pants, cupping my pussy and letting his fingertips brush against my swollen lips. "Baz." It'd been too long since a man touched me like this and even longer since the right man had. "Oh Baz," I moaned as one finger and then two slipped inside. My pussy clenched and flooded with moisture, letting his fingers slide faster and deeper until I cried out and moved against his hand.

"Yeah Sweetness, I want you to come. Come all over my hand, leave it sticky and wet." He pumped fast and hard bringing me closer and closer to orgasm and then he stopped.

"What the fuck Baz?"

"Sorry babe, I need more." He yanked down my shorts and panties, pulling off my bra and tank top before standing back to look me over. "Fuck you're so goddamn sexy." He dropped down on his knees and pulled me to the edge of the bed, palming my thighs to spread me indecently wide. "There's that pretty pink pussy I missed," he groaned, drawing close to inhale the scent of my arousal. He licked me over and over, long and slow from my asshole to my clit and back down. My gaze transfixed by his slow movements, his hungry gaze.

Then his tongue slipped inside me and I floated into another dimension. "Fuck Baz, yeah. Oh yes!" His tongue never ceased to amaze me. He worked me over hard, sucking and nibbling my clit, slurping noises that should have embarrassed me, but only turned me on even more.

Pulling my clit into his mouth, Baz sucked and hummed causing a deep vibration that yanked my orgasm right out of my body. It came hard and fast and violent and Baz wouldn't let it end, licking and sucking until I let out a keening wail that echoed off the walls. Finally, he slowed and then stopped, laughing but his lips still touched mine, sending another wave of vibrations through me. "Fuck I've missed this pussy. Sweetest ever."

Such a sweet talker. But, I didn't need—or want—the sweet talker. Fuck no. I wanted the foul-mouthed dirty talker who could make me come with just his words. "Baz."

"Yeah?"

"Shut the hell up and fuck me."

He stood and removed his clothes, letting me get my fill and hot damn the man looked better than ever.

There was more ink and more muscles and it all formed one sexy package that made me happy to spread my legs for him. "Whatever you want."

Perfect. "Hard. Fast. And dirty."

He gripped my ankles, letting his hands glide up and down until my whole body buzzed with desire. Everywhere he touched heated my skin, bringing me even closer to another orgasm. I knew there was a possibility I was going to hell for this, but Baz was always the one poison I couldn't resist.

"Hard," he said as he stroked his cock, his eyes searing through me. "Fast." His cock slipped in deep, drawing a hiss from me as my body clenched to get used to the way he filled me up but I remembered. Oh, I remembered all nine inches of him to perfection. "How do you want your dirty, Sweetness? You want me to tell you how I'm gonna fuck this pussy until you come all over me?"

His hips moved away from me and he slammed in oh so hard, my next orgasm waited just out of reach. "Or do you want me to make you my dirty girl all over again," he asked, licking his middle finger and playing at my ass like he used to.

"Yes Baz," I panted like a horny little hussy.

"Tell me Trina."

I grinned up at him. "I want all the dirty Baz. All of it."

"That's my girl," he groaned as his thick finger slid slowly into my ass while his cock pumped inside of me, harder and faster, so deep I could do little more than pant and scream as he fucked me so good every inch of my body was on fire.

"Baz, yes! Fuck me harder!" Another strangled groan escaped as he grunted, hips moving like a machine, a piston pumping hard and deep, his finger doing the same thing to my ass. "Baz," I moaned when he bent over, taking a nipple in his mouth and pulling hard, sucking as his teeth grazed the hard tip. And then I was falling from somewhere high above the earth, shouting and screaming my release as my hips moved in rhythm with his, giving him every fucking thing I had until I did exactly as he said I would. Hard and fast, and so dirty my pussy leaked all over his cock, milking him as he stroked.

"Fuck, Sweetness. So goddamn good," he grunted as hot, hard spurts of come splashed inside of me, mixing with my own juices. His hips continued to move, slow and deep while I rode out the rest of another orgasm. "Shit baby, I don't remember you being so orgasmic."

"It's been too long Baz, and you never disappoint. Not ever."

"Damn right I don't." He thrust again, shuddering over me. "You feel so good I want to stay right here and fuck you all night."

I was good with that. Tomorrow the regrets could come but right now, I would revel in the way he made me feel. "Who's stopping you?"

***

"Uh oh, pizza, wings and soda," Jack grimaced and eyed the food on the table suspiciously. "These are all my favorite things which means it's bad news."

"Hey!" I stared at him in disbelief. "Are you saying I only get you good stuff when I have bad news?" Who in the hell knew how he'd take this news but I assumed he'd be all right since he seemed to like Baz.

"No...but Mom, come on."

I rolled my eyes at him and finished dressing the salad. "Go get washed up so we can eat. Then talk." My body was still on fire from spending the afternoon in bed with Baz and I could hardly think straight, much less about all three of us sitting around the table like a happy family. Exactly how I always imagined it yet nothing at all how I thought it'd be with Baz and I fucking like casual strangers and Jack so in love with him he was bound to get his heart broken.

"It's going to be okay Trina." Baz's deep voice reassured me even if I didn't want it to.

"You don't know that. He's excited now because you're new and cool with your tattoos and motorcycle, but when he has time to think about it he'll feel differently." Hell, he'd probably hate me and after what Jensen put us through I couldn't even blame him.

"How?"

"That's the question Baz. He might hate me or you, he might hate both of us. Or he could act like every other man on the planet and bury his feelings deep until one day they all come out in the worst possible way." It was my worst fear, losing Jack. For so long it had just been me and him. Losing that would kill me.

"I call dibs on the extra hot sauce!" Jack slid into his seat effortlessly, grabbing food and pouring soda like it was just any other day.

"How was class?" Baz posed the question looking nothing but interested in the answer.

"So cool. CJ taught us all about how to check the car's computer with this little machine. But it costs too much for me to get one." He sounded so dejected I wanted to laugh.

"That's okay, I think I can afford to have it looked at. But if CJ doesn't mind helping you guys can do it together."

"I can do it," Baz offered up, an angry glare on his face.

"Really? Cool, right Mom?"

How could I look at those big green eyes and not agree? "Very cool." I half listened to him talk cars with Baz who smiled and added his knowledge, making our son smile. The pizza sat like lead in my belly as they talked sports and books and music, like old buddies. I'd deprived them both of this connection for all these years. Would it be like this from now on, Baz and Jack talking and me on the outside wishing I could get back in?

"What do you think Mom?"

I sighed and stared from one set of green eyes to another. "I think it's time we had that talk."

"About my dad?" he asked expectantly, his gaze flicking with uncertainty to Baz who remained stoic.

"Yes, about your father." I took a deep breath and looked my son right in the eyes. "Jack, before you were born, Baz and I dated for a few years and we were living together for a long time. We wanted different things in life so we broke up and I left town before I knew I was going to have a baby. Baz didn't know because I never spoke to him again, until I saw him at the diner." Eleven years ago, it sounded so right, so noble, but now it just sounded like bullshit excuses. I ran away from what could have been because I was scared.

Jack looked at Baz, his voice shaky when he spoke. "Do you want to be my dad, Baz?" He looked so hopeful, his heart in his eyes as he stared at the man who'd helped conceive him.

"Do I want to be your dad? Are you kidding me? I want nothing more in this world." With his voice laced with emotion, Baz pushed his chair back and held his arms out. His shoulders drooped in relief when Jack stepped into his arms and squeezed him for all he was worth.

The moment would be seared into my heart, my mind and my soul for the rest of my life. I couldn't change the past but I could change the future and make sure they had the relationship they should've had all these years.

Chapter Five

Baz

"The key to a good burger is press the center with your thumb to make sure it gets perfectly done." Somehow, I was back at Trina's place for dinner yet again. Tonight we grilled outside and I was manning the grill, teaching Jack the secrets every man knew. Like a real fucking father.

It was surreal.

"What about the sausages?"

The kid looked at me like I knew everything, had all the answers. It was overwhelming but it also filled something in me I didn't even know was missing. The kid asked a lot of questions and I tried my best to answer them all. After he ripped my heart out when he asked if I wanted to be his dad, I went home and spent the rest of the night making damn sure I could be the man he needed in his life. I woke up the next day and asked Trina if he could spend the day with me. It was sweet fucking heaven ever since. "Sausages are easy. They take no time to cook so it depends on how you like 'em. When we were young your mom used to like them a little burnt."

"She still does," he answered with a disgusted turn of his nose.

"Good, because she did all the cooking and that's still how I like 'em." That was true and sad but I had to be honest with the kid.

"Can you make two normal?"

"Sure thing, kid." Damn that smile gutted me every single time. "Everything is all done so let's grub." We sat at the red picnic table in the backyard, me and Jack on one side and Trina on the other, just watching us. She hadn't said much since I arrived but she didn't seem sad or angry, just watchful. Contemplative. "Is this your famous potato salad?"

"Why's it famous Mom?"

"It's not but in case you haven't noticed your dad has a hollow leg." She made the same joke she'd made after every meal. At Jack's look of confusion, she explained. "Because he can put away so much food."

His face brightened and he turned to me with a familiar smile that was all Trina. "Like my tapeworm?"

"Your what?"

"Mom says I have a tapeworm in my belly helping me eat so much."

I had to laugh at that. "Yep, exactly like that. Let's show her how we do it." With a determined look, Jack and I ate like it was our last meal. It was fun, watching Trina watch us like two aliens who'd landed in her life.

Finally she'd apparently had enough of our shenanigans, pulling away the platter of meat and two bowls filled with food. "If either one of you eat any more food I promise I will make you regret it."

Jack giggled and Trina glared but I just laughed. They were silly and ridiculous and I was having the time of my fucking life. "I'm stuffed Jack, how about you?"

"Couldn't eat another bite," he patted his stomach with a conspiratorial grin.

"How about we hit up Two Scoops for dessert?"

"I love chocolate and mint chocolate chip!"

In all my life, I'd never seen someone so excited about ice cream and I loved it. "I want one of those hot caramel sundaes. What about you Sweetness, what are you having?"

She sighed, gathering every ounce of patience she could find within her and grinned. "Frozen yogurt."

"Ew, Mom. Gross."

"Yeah, Sweetness, totally gross."

She stood. "I need to change while you two piglets deal with this," she gestured to the table and sauntered off, my eyes glued to her long legs and round ass.

Even with my son right beside me, my cock twitched with the need to slide deep inside her again. "Ew, Dad. Gross."

Dad. He called me Dad. "What? She's beautiful."

He glared, arms crossed over his shirt. "She's my mom."

"She's not my mom," I told him as we gathered dishes and tossed plastic forks and paper plates in the trash. I didn't have to wonder what Jack thought about it because the kid had no filter.

"It's okay if you want to date her. You treat her nice and I think she likes you too."

"You do?"

He nodded, blonde hair flopping over his eyes. "Yep. She does that tiny smile thing with her eyes when she looks at you."

"You're making that up." But I couldn't help but laugh at the kid scrunching his eyes up. "What you're doing doesn't look like you like me, it looks like you're having a seizure."

He laughed as we finished putting food away and went inside where Trina waited for us, looking good enough to eat in a little summer dress. "Are we ready?"

With a quick nod, we all took off down the street, making the short journey to the ice cream shop owned by Trudy, the ol' lady of one of my CAOS brothers. I was surprised to find Dagger there with their three kids. I took Jack to meet the oldest boy Teddy, while Trina placed our orders inside.

"So, a kid huh?" Dagger hit me with that sly grin he always wore as we watched Teddy and Jack take turns on the lone skateboard between them.

"Yep. Found out she was pregnant after she'd left my ass."

"Why is she back now?" Fuck. I thought all about that little shit brick Jensen and told Dagger about it. "Said she thought I might be dead by now, only came back to get away from that prick."

"That kid makes them both family. She know that?"

I shrugged because I had no fucking clue. We hadn't bothered talking about it, probably because we were both eager to avoid that particular argument. "She knows I'll protect them both."

Dagger stared at me, eyes hard and determined. "*We'll* protect them, you mean."

I nodded because that's how it worked, whether Trina wanted it to or not. "Thanks Sweetness. You know Dagger?" She took the seat across from us, enjoying her frozen yogurt.

"Trudy's husband, right? Nice to see you again." She was stiff and uncertain, telling me she had no plans to get used to my club.

Dagger sent me a look and I knew exactly what he was thinking. A woman who wasn't okay with the club wouldn't last long with a man whose life was the club. "Yeah I know."

Dagger stood and frowned. "Incoming," he whispered and walked away. Fucking coward.

"Hey Baz, you sexy devil, where the hell ya been?"

Oh no. This *pass-around* was the most persistent of them all, never taking no for an answer and no issues with trying to steal someone else's guy. Bleached blonde hair, big fake tits and long, scrawny legs tottered my way and I didn't have to look back to know Trina had also noticed. "I've been around."

"I haven't seen you," she pouted, devil-red lips ripe and ready for a blow job. *If* I was interested in what she was offering. "In ages."

"Maybe I'm not looking to be found." Firm and direct usually worked but Pam wasn't interested in being shoved off. Not if there was still a chance for her to become someone's ol' lady. "What do you want Pam?"

"I want you Baz. How long are you gonna make me wait? You know I'll do anything." She pressed her tits up against me, pouting harder when I stepped away from her and that nasty ass perfume. "Anything."

"What part of—"

"We're heading out," Trina began, a blank expression on her face, "and Jack wanted to say bye." She stepped back when I reached out for her, letting

Jack step in between us and telling me how she felt about me and Pam. Even though there was no fucking *me and Pam.*

"See ya later, Dad!" He waved nervously and then went for it, wrapping his scrawny arms around my waist and squeezing hard.

"Later, kid. Trina." Without a word, not a single expression on her face, she turned away and I knew I'd be starting over again with her. "Goddammit Pam I told you I'm not interested in what you're offering."

She grinned. "I can make you interested."

I shook my head. "And I can make you sorry if you don't back the fuck off." I hated being harsh with women but she'd just fucked shit up for me and I wasn't in the mood to be kind.

"Fine. You're not such hot shit anyway." I saw it for the defensive gesture it was but fixed my face into an expression that told her how serious I was.

"Then move the fuck on," I barked at her and went back inside Two Scoops where Dagger wrangled his kids like an expert. I had a shit load of questions for the club's resident family man.

***

"What do you want Baz?" Trina stood in the doorway with her arms folded, her expression cool and distant. Still.

A week had passed and though she hadn't made any attempts to keep me away from Jack she hadn't gone out of her way to speak to me or let me in again. I flashed the smile she never used to be able to resist but so much had changed about Trina over the years. Dammit. "I was hoping we could talk."

She stepped back, her gaze still cold, but she moved warily away from me and took one of two solo seats in her living room, arms and legs crossed defensively. "What is it you want to talk about?"

Shit, where did I begin? I had so much to apologize for before I figured the beginning was as good a place as any. "I wanted to apologize about before. Back then. I had no idea how much my life in the club scared you. I was a young punk and all I could see was my woman trying to control me. I didn't see what you were trying to tell me." I was too young and too set on joining CAOS to be able to listen anyway.

She sighed and ran a trembling hand through her hair. "We both made our choices Baz and I really don't see a point in going over it again. You know about Jack now and he's thrilled to have you around so we should just move forward." I would've believed her if her whole expression, her whole body hadn't been wrapped up in a posture that said get the hell away from me.

"How do you propose we do that?"

She sighed. "Simple. Spend time with Jack like you've been doing. Here, for a few weeks and when you both are comfortable you can keep him over night. If that's what you want."

Who was this cold, formal creature determined to piss me off? "*If* I want? What the fuck does that mean Trina? You know I want to be involved, more than anything." I stood and closed the distance between us until I towered over her. "Fine. I'll come back tonight for dinner." Since there were no classes this week thanks to the upcoming Fourth of July holiday, I could come early and stay all day. "In the meantime—" I told her, stepping closer when she stood to face me, deftly dodging my touch.

"—I think you have enough women to keep you busy, to warm your bed Baz. Just focus on Jack."

I heard what she was saying and what she wasn't but that didn't bother me. Grabbing her chin and tilting her head up, I made sure those pretty blue eyes looked right into mine. "Just like you haven't been celibate all these years Trina, neither have I. But now the only woman I can think about is you, Sweetness. So get that through your pretty little head."

Her hands went to my chest to push me away but I gripped her forearms and kept her close. "We have both lived our lives Baz and our encounter the other day probably gave you the wrong impression. I don't sleep around and I don't do it casually."

But I did, at least according to her unspoken rebuke. "Well, just an FYI, I didn't fuck Pam. Never have. Not interested." Couldn't she see the only woman on my mind anymore was her? "My cock only wants you Trina."

She opened her mouth to respond but I slipped inside with my tongue, teasing and tasting her, devouring her sweet hot mouth until every inch of me throbbed with the need to slide deep inside her tight, wet cunt. But not now. "Remember that," I told her roughly and walked out.

I needed to put some space between us, so I hopped on my bike and headed toward the clubhouse. These guys were my friends, my brothers and with them was exactly where I needed to be right now.

"What's up?" I walked in to find Torch, Mick and Cash congregated around the bar having a conversation that looked too damn serious for this early in the day.

Mick turned with a frown dipping his red brows low. "What's up is Wagman's been spotted in town."

Shit. "Wagman? I thought that motherfucker was dead." I thought we'd seen the last of that fucker. He'd disappeared after the shit went down with Rocky and the Devils, and I, *we* hoped it was for good. Now though, it appeared he was just lying low.

"He's been freelancing for all manner of criminals. Wet work, enforcement, security you name it and he's been up to it. The fact he's back means someone probably paid him. For something," he added ominously.

Instantly my mind went to Trina's ex. "Jensen something or fucking other. He's locked up in Connecticut for some financial crimes. I don't know the details but he and Trina dated for a few months several years ago and he's been stalking her ever since. If that asshole hired Wagman I'll do my best to make sure both men regret it." I went quiet for a second, thinking about my kid. I had to make sure he and Trina were both protected from these clowns.

I was pulled from my thoughts and looked up to find three sets of eyes staring at me in various stages of shock. "Oh, and I have a kid. His name is Jack and he's ten years old."

Calm descended for about five seconds before the men erupted in cheers, whistles and slaps of congratulations on the back. "That's a reason to fuckin' celebrate!" Torch clapped my back, shaking me in excitement, smiling widely. "Congratulations man, this is fucking unreal!" The big man hugged me hard and lifted me off the ground, giving my back a solid pounding.

We cracked open a keg of beer and a few bottles of Jack and I sat through a few toasts and plenty of ribbing about missing the hard years. I took all the jokes with a smile because these guys were my family and I knew they'd step up to help me with Jack and Trina, and with whatever the fuck Wagman was doing back in Brently. "How you holding up?" Mick took a seat beside me with a slow, easy grin.

"As good as a man in my position could be, I suppose." I was happy to find out about Jack and getting to know him made me feel things I never thought I would. And even having Trina back in my life had changed things for me, but I couldn't deny a certain hint of anger of what had been stolen from me all those years ago. I missed watching her belly grow round with our child. Missed seeing Jack losing his teeth, learning to ride a bike and all the other shit fathers are supposed to be around for.

"She had her reasons, same as Talon's mother did. Doesn't make it right but at least you found out about Jack before it's too late. Magnus didn't get that chance."

"You had to go there, didn't you man?"

Mick grinned and took a long sip from the frosty mug. "Yep. Eats up Talon every day that she never got to meet him, especially now that we have our own kids."

"So, forgive and forget and then move forward?"

"Pretty much. It's all you can do, or you can let your anger get the better of you and push them both away." Mick stood and knocked his mug against mine. "Your choice."

I stewed over his words, knocking back a few beers and a few more shots as everyone made their way over to offer me advice, congrats and more booze. Mick had a point. Being pissed off about the situation wouldn't magically turn back time and change anything, but if I let Trina see me that way, it might change the present. The future.

"Smile man, I know you hated it when Trina left." Torch grinned in my fucking face, refusing to let me sulk in my booze.

"Yeah I did hate it but now I fucking hate that I didn't pay more attention to what she said back then." That's the part that stuck with me. "She was trying to tell me about her fear but I wouldn't listen. And she left."

"But she's fucking here now Baz, that's the part that matters. This is your chance, don't be an asshole. Be a man."

"Fuck you Torch."

The crazy fucker laughed. "Nah you're not my type. I like my ladies with bigger tits."

Torch had a point though. Trina is the only woman other than Cherie I'd let get close to me and her leaving fucked me up. Bad. But now that she's back, I could have it all. The cool as shit son. The hot chick. But first I had to earn her trust and maybe her love again. *Fuck, I must be drunk if I'm thinking about love.* I didn't talk—or think—about love other than my sister and my club. "Prospect get me some water. And some coffee." I couldn't get too damn drunk because I promised Trina I'd be back for dinner and I wasn't about to show up shitfaced.

I needed to show her that what she thought about CAOS wasn't reality. We weren't a bunch of fucking criminals. We were men who'd served our country with honor and distinction, but that service had given us a glimpse of how the real world fucking worked. So we made our own rules and our own lives. Our way. The outlaw way.

I drank two cups of coffee fast enough to burn my fucking tongue but I needed to get going. After dropping my bike off at home, I grabbed my truck and headed to the grocery store. I had just the thing to warm Trina a little and get on my son's good side. A sundae bar for after dinner.

If I could survive basic training and several tours in the fucking shithole known as the middle east, then I could get one little strawberry blonde to open up to me.

Again.

Chapter Six

Trina

Since Jack was home all week, Baz had been spending plenty of time at the house which meant I could spend more time working on my novel. He'd stopped by earlier, offering to take Jack to the park a couple of blocks away so I could get some work done. I appreciated that because I'd had too many late nights over the past few weeks. I couldn't deny the progress I'd made and it was all thanks to the same man responsible for my sleepless nights.

Even though I refused to sleep with him again—no matter how much I wanted to—he'd been in my thoughts a lot. So much that my hero started to look and act like him—the heat between my characters resembled the heat between us whenever we were together. Every time he stopped by I couldn't help replaying the hard and fast fuck we'd had. In my bed.

The sound of the doorbell pulled me from my thoughts, wondering what kind of distraction would stop my progress now. "Delivery for Trina Mosley," the friendly looking man said, handing me a bouquet of what looked to be two dozen red roses.

I hated red roses with a passion. They were phony. Insincere. And I knew only one person who would send them, despite how I felt. "Thanks," I told the kid and waved him off, dumping the flowers in the trash and slipping the card into the kitchen junk drawer. The card wouldn't provide any evidence it was Jensen but I kept it anyway and went back to work.

Unfortunately, back to work meant delving back into thoughts I'd rather forget because they always turned to Baz and his capable hands, hard lines and muscles, intoxicating mouth. Though I'd never been into drugs, Baz had always been my one true addiction. But I had to shake off thoughts of him even if they were helping me finish my novel because it also made me want him more than I should. More than I could afford to want him when I knew nothing could come of it.

Because nothing *could* come of it. Nothing had changed. Baz still belonged to CAOS, was probably some kind of leader at this point and though I hadn't seen any evidence of criminal activity yet, I couldn't rule it out either. Which meant I couldn't let toe-curling amazing sex or anything else soften me towards him or the idea of us.

The doorbell rang again and I pushed back from my desk with a grunt at another damn interruption. A quick glance out the window revealed a strange man with long greasy brown hair and light blue eyes with a scar under the left eye. He looked dirty and mean so I pulled open the door cautiously, keeping the knob gripped in one hand. "How may I help you?"

"You Trina Mosley," he asked gruffly.

"Depends on who's asking and why." Though I already had a feeling I knew exactly who'd sent this miscreant to my door.

He stepped closer, grinning sinisterly when I stepped back. "Just someone offering up some helpful advice sugar."

"Yeah and what would that be?"

He sneered, reaching out a hand to try and touch me. "When Jensen calls, take it or your boy might find himself in a really fucked up situation."

I stood, shaken and pale as he walked away, fucking whistling as he walked down the street. As soon as the man was out of my line of sight I grabbed the phone and dialed Baz. "Come back here. Now!"

"Calm down Sweetness, what's—"

"—Now, Baz!" Still clutching the phone, I ran outside and up the block, thinking I'd meet them in the middle of the block. I spotted them soon enough with Baz's casual amble and ran to them, wrapping Jack in my arms.

"Ow Mom, too tight." He groaned and stepped back, looking at me like I'd grown two heads.

"Sorry baby." I felt tears threatening but I knew they would scare Jack more than my behavior already had.

"Trina what the hell is going on? Tell me what's wrong," he insisted as he pulled me up from the ground and wrapped an arm around my waist. He herded us both into the house.

"Mom, what's going on? Is it Jensen again?"

I remained silent and went straight to the kitchen, pulling the grinder forward and dumping in coffee beans to keep my hands occupied. "Jack can you go to your room for a bit so I can talk to your father?"

"Mo-o-om," he whined.

"I've called Dagger and he's coming to pick up Jack," he told me, sympathy shining in his eyes. "This way Jack has someone to hang out with while Dagger keeps an eye on him. So we can talk."

I wanted to argue, to tell him he had no damn right to make those decisions without me. But he was right—and he was his father. Dagger would treat Jack as though he was his own son, because as far as the club was concerned it was true. "Okay. Thanks. How does that sound Jack?"

"Okay," he mumbled. "Are you gonna be all right Mom?"

"Yep."

"I'll make sure of it," Baz told him, placing a comforting hand on his shoulder. Treating him like the man he would become someday. Thirty minutes later Jack was gone and Baz turned to me. "What the hell happened?"

I took a long chug of lukewarm coffee and let out a deep breath before I told him everything I could remember about the man, his words and the earlier delivery of the roses. He bit out a curse and I frowned as a cold sensation snaked through me. "You know him?"

"Sounds like Wagman. He used to be a member but he and a few other guys killed one of our members, remember Magnus?"

I nodded. "Of course. He was nice, owned Black Betty and always had a smile for everyone."

"Well they fucking killed him and we had to expel them. Some shit went down, and I honestly thought the fucker was dead, but I just found out the other day that he's doing freelance work." He bit out the words like they stung to say. "I'll find him and shut this shit down Sweetness, I promise."

I knew he would but I couldn't stop trembling. "He threatened Jack, Baz. I can't have anyone threatening my son."

"Our son," he corrected angrily.

"Maybe I should just talk to Jensen, take his call."

He grabbed me and held me close, resting his chin on my head while I inhaled his strong leathery masculine scent. "Fuck no. Don't let this asshole win Trina. You don't want to talk to him then keep doing that. I assume you have a restraining order?"

I nodded. "But I don't know if it works across state lines or if the phone counts." The clerk, the cops and even the judge hadn't been all that helpful.

"Doesn't matter. Just don't talk to him. Ignore the bastard." His grasp was firm at first but then it gentled as a finger traced along my hairline and down to my jaw before coming to a stop under my chin. "I'm moving in."

I shook my head. "That is a really bad idea Baz."

"It's a damn good idea and you know it. I'm the best option of keeping you both safe. Who'll do a better job of it than me?"

Shit, he was right. With Jack tying us together, Baz would move heaven and hell to keep him safe. But still, I wasn't ready for that. "You don't need to live here to keep us safe, do you?"

"Yeah? Because trust me when I tell you that Wag is a desperate man who will do just about any fucking thing for the right price. Nighttime is the best time to strike and that's when you'll be most vulnerable without me here."

"No!"

"Goddammit Trina, stop being so stubborn."

"This is my house Baz and you can't just move in because you feel like it." I didn't even know why I was fighting him so hard. I knew it was the best option but I couldn't *not* fight it. Having him so close and all the time would make it hard to keep my distance.

Baz crowded me and I pushed at his chest, drawing a deep laugh from him. "Don't worry Trina, I won't come to you unless you beg me to. And Sweetness, you *will* beg."

Why did that deep sexy voice soak my panties and make my pussy clench? Because this man just did it for me. Every. Damn. Time. "I doubt it."

He used his big body against me, pressing me into the wall so I could feel his cock hardening against me. Then he slanted his mouth across mine, devouring my hot breath until I could no longer tell where his breath stopped and mine started. I could only succumb to the pleasure that filled my mouth and radiated down my body until everything tingled, buzzed with a need to feel more of this man. Touch and taste more of him. I moaned into his mouth and he pulled back, hands speared through my hair. "Still doubt me?"

"Not you, exactly," I stammered out to his answering chuckle.

"Well then, I'm happy to convince you."

I shouldn't encourage him, but with his hands on me, his body pressed into mine, I couldn't resist. "You're welcome to try."

And that was all he needed to put those big hands on my ass and lift me, urging my legs to wrap around his waist which I did happily, groaning at the feel of his cock pressed right where I needed it to be. Long legs ate up the distance to my bedroom where he laid me out and slowly undressed me, with a sinful grin that lit up his handsome face. "Open up Trina." That gritty commanding tone had my arousal already dripping down my thighs. "Now."

I put my feet on the bed and spread my legs, pulsing at his heated look.

"Better. You're so fucking beautiful, Sweetness. I'm gonna eat that pussy until you can't feel your legs."

Yes please, was the only thing I could think of at that moment. No one lit my body up like Baz did and right now, I felt like I might float away any minute. He knelt between my thighs and instead on moving nice and slow like I thought he might, he dove in fast and hard, alternating between fucking me with his tongue and sucking on my clit. "Baz, please!" I cried his name over and over, clutching his hair and grinding against his mouth.

"Can't hear you," he groaned, nibbling my clit before I could get another word out.

The sensations shook me, rattled my body from my head to my toes and then I flew apart, shattering while his mouth continued to make me feel *oh so good*. Then it became too much and I couldn't control my limbs and Baz kept up steady strokes of his tongue on my clit. "Baz," I panted out to get his attention.

"I'm not done with you yet," he growled and stood, pulling my legs until they hung off the bed and spinning me like a rag doll. "How long this lasts depends on how fast you come."

Though upside down I watched, fascinated as he undressed but kept his gaze on my tits as he did it. Deciding to do a little teasing of my own, I let one hand snake between my legs and watched his gaze track my hand as it landed on my clit, the flicking motion making me swell, the sound of the moisture making his cock grow. Then he was gloriously naked and stroking his cock and my mouth watered. Baz smiled when I licked my lips and stood in front of me, his cock in licking distance so I did just that.

"Open up Trina."

I obeyed his command and his cock filled my mouth as his bodyweight pressed me into the bed and then his mouth was there again, slurping at my pussy as he fucked my mouth. Filling me deliciously from both ends all I could do was use my mouth to make him groan, make his hips change their speed and depth. With his cock in my mouth it took no time at all for another orgasm to tear through me, spearing my throat with his thick length.

"Fuck, that mouth feels even better than I remember." I could hear the smile in his voice as he stood again, thrusting a few more times down my throat before stepping back.

"Where are you going?"

"I'm about to be balls deep inside you. Any objections?"

Hell no. "None." I spun and opened my legs obscenely wide, loving the way his green eyes flared with desire at the sight of my pussy. I cried out when he filled me in one quick thrust and froze, letting his cock pulse and thicken inside me. "Baz."

"Fuck Trina, you feel so good."

"Move, please." I urged him, digging my heels into his ass.

"The sound of you begging for my cock makes me so fucking hard, Sweetness."

I smiled up at him. "Then *please* Baz. Fuck me."

"All you had to do was ask." He slid out and lifted my legs higher, sliding deeper with the new angle and every thought flew from my mind except the feel of his hard cock pounding into me, stretching me out. Hard and fast, he fed his cock into me over and over, the sounds of my pleasure and slick skin smacking together, igniting a raw hunger in him that I'd never experienced.

He gave everything and I did the same in return, raking my nails down his back as he drove deeper and deeper, growling when I licked up his neck and then bit down on his shoulder. "Fuuuck!"

His hips moved at warp speed, reminding me of the last time we made love, the time that we conceived Jack and the past merged with the present as I flew into a million tiny pieces, squeezing and milking him as his last strokes came with more force, more passion than the previous ones. "Oh Baz, yes!"

Moments later he followed me over the edge, freezing deep inside me, jerking out his orgasm and collapsing beside me. Holding me close. "Damn that was...,"

"Yeah. It was," I told him and swiped my tongue across his hard, flat nipple. "You still can't move in."

He laughed. "I already have."

"It wouldn't set a good example for Jack and worse, it'll get his hopes up that we're getting back together." I knew having him around would provide additional protection but I had to think about Jack. About me. My heart.

Baz flipped our positions and pinned me underneath him, grinding his cock against my swollen folds. "This isn't about us Sweetness but make no mistake, there is an us. There will *be* an us," he punctuated his words with a thrust of his hips, making it hard to concentrate which was his plan. "Soon," he growled and dotted kisses across my neck, my jaw. My mouth. "But this is about keeping you both safe. I'm highly motivated, uniquely qualified for the job. So, say yes Trina."

"No."

Licking his lips hypnotically he moved his hips so his cock stamped right on my clit, drawing a satisfied hiss from me. "I can make you say yes."

"You can try," I told him around a moan, locking my legs low on his back. His huge cock slipped inside me and he groaned.

"I fully plan to try," he pulled his hips back and slammed in. Deep. "And I plan to succeed." He did it again. "But this is about keeping you and our son safe." And again. "And I know that's what you want above all else."

Dammit he was right.

Still, I let him spend the next few hours wringing an enthusiastic yes from me.

***

"Oh. My. God. Are you serious?" Talon's big silver eyes were wild and wide with excitement. "You're Teagan Chantilly?"

I nodded with a shy smile. I so rarely shared my romance author alter ego with anyone and these women were all fans. Big fans. "That's the name I've used to publish my books."

Minx and Kyla both squealed, drawing odd looks from some of the guys and a few other tables filled with people I hadn't yet met. "You must have the greatest fuckin' sex life on the planet," Kyla said with confidence.

I shook my head, smiling and wondering how in the hell I'd let Baz and Jack convince me spending the Fourth of July with his motorcycle gang was a good idea. "Not much, really. I've had quite a few first dates and one relationship that lasted long enough for him to meet my son. Mostly this is fantasy." And a lot was memory but I couldn't possibly share that with these women. Not yet. "Anyway, I'd appreciate it if you could keep my secret. I worry about how Jack's friends and their parents would react if they knew."

"Your secret is safe with us," Trudy assured me. "Now, where's my Kindle?" She laughed.

"Girl you have no idea how lucky Mick got during my first pregnancy because of your books. I swear I think I got pregnant with my second while I was still pregnant with my first," Talon joked, fanning her flawless face.

Hearing how much people loved my books always thrilled me, but especially these women who I figured would likely become good friends in the months to come. "Then I'd love it if you ladies could spare a few nights a year to be my beta readers."

Talon nodded enthusiastically while Minx asked when the next book would be ready. "All I can do now is read so I'm your girl."

I smiled in gratitude and wondered if I could pick their brains about some of the things on my mind. "I was wondering—"

"Hey ladies, how's it going?" Cash strolled up looking boyishly handsome as he pressed a kiss to his wife's cheek. "How you doin' babe?"

Minx beamed a loving smile his way that made me envy her and that kind of love. "Fat and hungry. Unless you want to stay for girl talk?"

He shook his head quickly, warning off Mick and Baz who were on their way over. Trudy laughed. "Works every time. I love these guys but they're terrified of female emotions." She settled back into her seat and crossed her legs. "You were wondering?" she prompted.

I sighed and let my gaze fall on each of them as I asked the question. "I was wondering how you all cope with CAOS and what they do, while still maintaining your families?"

"I had my doubts about Dagger as well, but he promised they didn't deal drugs or hookers and they only do what needs to be done." Trudy's gaze was strong and steady. "It's not as bad as you think, and when the shit hits the fan, these guys will protect us all with their lives."

"That's been my experience," Talon said and went on to explain how she hid Dagger in a hidden wall when ex-club members had come after him.

I couldn't believe my ears. "Seriously?"

She nodded towards Minx who agreed and told me all about how Wagman had come after her and the club rode to her rescue while she and Talon were chased on the highway. "Plus, Magnus saved me from a life of forced prostitution."

Shit. "Forced prostitution? That's bad, really bad." Her story brought tears to my eyes as I thought of the life she would've had if the club hadn't intervened. "I don't mean to offend any of you but I had no idea when I left Brently what CAOS was other than a motorcycle gang."

"Club," they all corrected in unison, making me smile.

"Listen girl, they mostly deal in guns and bikes, both of which are legal in California...mostly," Kyla said with a twist of her face. "But many of these guys have individual interests as well. Mick owns the gas station and auto shop and Cash invests in some dispensaries. Even Baz has a lucrative business on the side."

That I didn't know but it wasn't my main concern. "What about the danger that comes to you because of their business dealings?"

"Honey, trouble comes either way," Trudy said plainly.

"That's true. I'm the one who brought it this time," I said in reply, the sympathy burning in Trudy's eyes was like a kick in the gut. Then, I told them about Wagman's visit to my door on behalf of my ex.

"You know, he used to be one of us," Minx said, shaking her head. "He betrayed the club and we all thought he was dead. Be careful," she warned. "He's mean, ruthless and he has no one to lean on which means he's dangerous as hell."

I nodded as I took in the information, my gaze straying to Jack who laughed and ran alongside Baz who carried a football under his arm. He really loved having a dad, especially one who was one hundred percent masculinity, alpha male goodness. They fell in love so quickly and I knew I couldn't deprive Baz of the chance to keep us safe.

"I guess he's moving in then," I said to the girls who all wore knowing grins. "Wipe those grins off your faces. He'll sleep on the sofa because I cannot fall in love with him again. The last time nearly killed me!" I feared I was, once again, halfway there.

"I said the same thing," Kyla laughed. "But weeks on end locked inside a mansion with Torch made that an impossible promise to keep."

"Ugh! Don't tell me that," I groaned. Each one of these women had her own story of falling for a biker against her better judgment, and so far, it had worked out well for each one of them. They all had children or were pregnant, were married or getting married. Above all, they were all happily in love.

Too bad I was too chicken shit to make that leap.

Chapter Seven

Baz

"I'll take the guestroom Sweetness just so you're not tempted to jump my bones. Again." I don't know what happened but after a day spent grilling at the clubhouse on the Fourth, Trina agreed to let me move in even though I could tell she still felt wary about the whole thing.

"There is no guestroom. The spare is my office and no one but me is allowed in there, got it?" I nodded, smirking at how sexy she looked all serious and fierce about her work. "You'll be sleeping on the sofa."

I looked at that sorry excuse for a couch and then back to Trina with skepticism. It was at least two feet too damn small and the twitch of her lips told me she knew it. "Guess we'll be sharing after all."

"Fine," she said with groan, shaking her head. "You take the bed and I'll take the sofa."

I reached out and grabbed her arm, pulling her close until we stood chest to chest. "You know I can't allow that, Sweetness. But I'll tell you what, we'll share a bed but I'll only sink my cock into that deliciously wet cunt of yours, if you ask real nice." She laughed but I saw the flash of desire in those deep blue eyes and I knew, if I slid a finger between her thighs she would be sticky and dripping all over my hand. No one got as wet as Trina did and even now my cock tightened at the thought.

We broke apart at the sound of Jack's door opening. "Are you really moving in Dad, for real?"

Damn it never got old hearing him call me that with the enthusiasm only a little kid can have. "For real. At least for a while anyway." I knew Trina only meant this to be temporary but I didn't plan to leave, at least not without my family.

"All right!" Jack punched the air, a smile lighting up his face as he flung his skinny frame—all arms and legs—at me and Trina. "This is super cool!"

It turned out the kid was right. Living with Trina and Jack was unlike anything I'd experienced in my own adult life. I had some memories of my own mom whipping up breakfast every morning the way Trina did for us, eggs and bacon some days, pancakes, waffles and even disgusting ass oatmeal. But I ate up every goddamned bite because there was something appealing as fuck watching a woman wake up early to nourish her family. I got to spend extra time with Jack by taking him to the community center each morning, which meant Trina got to spend more time working in her office. She never said what she worked on and I hadn't asked her but I would.

Soon.

It was all so fucking domestic and that was something I'd told myself I never wanted again, not after I'd come home five days after the fight that sent Trina running from me and Brently. This. We could have had *this* for the past ten years but we were both too young and immature to fight for it. To fight for *us*. This time though I wouldn't give up so easily.

***

"What about tacos?" Jack held up both soft and hard shells with a bright grin that reminded me so much of my younger self.

"You want to make tacos?" I had the dumb idea that me and the kid could make dinner tonight and let Trina work until she tired herself out. Now though I was having doubts because tacos were a whole lot of shit and I was more of the grill a slab a meat and whip up some instant mashed potatoes kind of guy.

He nodded. "Me and Mom make them on Fridays with all the toppings."

All the toppings. Sounded like a fuck ton of work to me but I couldn't look at the face and say no. "All right. What do we need?" I pushed the cart while Jack named all kinds of shit we would need like lettuce and olives. "Olives? You sure?"

He laughed, bobbing his head up and down and squeezing fifty tomatoes before putting eight in a bag.

"Mom says you have to make sure they're soft but not too soft."

"My sister makes the best salsa around. Hot as fuck but good." Shit. I cringed at his wide-eyed smile. "Sorry."

"It's fine. I promised Mom I'd wait until my vocabulary improved before I started using them." He said it so matter of fact I knew Trina had done a good job with the kid.

"Good. But uhm, maybe don't tell your Mom." He nodded his agreement, his attention already back to the ingredients we would need. "Are these gourmet tacos?"

"Nope." Thank fuck twenty minutes later we stood in the kitchen unpacking the bags while Trina stayed holed up in her office. "Mom must be in the zone," Jack commented as he pulled out the cheese grater and set up the way I guessed he and Trina did before I got here.

"What's she doing in there?" I knew she had a blog, Minx had told me as much but that seemed like more work than just kid shit for moms.

"Working. She has a blog she started when I was a kid, that helps other moms do cool things for their kids even if they can't afford it. She always did cool things like that for me growing up, making cakes and stuff." He smiled at the memory that was like a punch in the balls for me, realizing she'd started this blog because as a single mother she couldn't afford do everything our son deserved. "Or she's working on her books, the ones I'm not supposed to know about."

Books? I wondered how a blog allowed her to pay all the bills a kid required but, books? "What kind of books?"

Jack shrugged. "They're for girls, well grown up girls and I'm not supposed to know about them so you should ask her."

Damn. Schooled by a fifth grader. "You're protective of her. That's good. A man should protect his family."

He nodded, seeming deep in thought. "It's always just been me and Mom. She works hard to give me everything I need and plenty of things I want. I just want her to be happy." He started grating an onion and dumping it in a bowl. "For the salsa," he said and rinsed the grater before tackling the cheese.

Shit this kid was the absolute fucking best. I would have to be a better man than I thought I could be. For him. "Okay what do I do?"

Jack walked me through what he could remember and the internet helped us with the rest. I couldn't deny helping out like this gave me a sense of accomplishment I never would've imagined, and Jack ate up everything I said like it was the fucking gospel.

"Man, what smells so good?"

"We cooked dinner Mom. Tacos!"

Suspiciously watery blue eyes widened as she took in the spread on the table. "You even made the salsa? Fantastic."

"Yeah well Jack said the jar stuff had a lot of sugar in it." Didn't make sense to me but I took the kid's word for it.

"Thank you guys. I was completely in the zone and sometimes that means we end up with takeout." She smiled at our son who rolled his eyes affectionately and wrapped an arm around her waist.

"It's nice to share the load then, isn't it?"

She nodded as she took a seat and began assembling a taco. "Delicious. How was your day kiddo?"

I sat back, listening as Jack told her all about the book he was reading about genius kids fighting crime in space. Sounded complicated as hell but he ate up the series like they were comic books. "I'm almost finished," he proudly declared.

"With another one? Wow you must want something pretty big this year," she told him casually.

"What?" Catching up on their shorthand took some time but I realized real fast that asking was the best way to find out.

Trina stood at the sound of the phone ringing but I grabbed her wrist as Jack explained, "Mom gives me five bucks for every book I read and summarize but instead of giving me the cash we total it and I get to buy whatever I want. As long as it's legal. And safe," he tacked on the last part with an eye roll that told me the kid had hidden depths.

"I'll get it," I told her, pulling her down and reaching for the cordless phone on the counter. "Hello?" My whole body tensed at the automated voice asking me if I wanted to accept the collect call. "Yes." As soon as the smarmy bastard started speaking I shut that shit down. "Listen to me you tiny dick motherfucker, if you call or send someone else to bother either of them, I'll make sure you spend the rest of your life eating through a motherfuckin' straw. Got it?" I didn't wait for a fucking response because if he called again or Wagman showed up, I'd make good on my promise. Trina looked at me with a mixture of worry and fear but Jack just looked proud. In awe. I just grinned to get rid of the tension in the air.

"So…who wants dessert?" Jack stood and went to the fridge with a wide smile.

Damn I loved my kid.

***

"Did you ever love Mom? Do you still love her?"

Damn the kid didn't pull any punches. "Your mom was the only woman I ever loved besides my sister and mom and I never stopped loving her. When you're young you want things how you want them and I was too stubborn to compromise. Trina and I couldn't, so she left." I'd kicked my own ass for months after she'd gone. Why had I stayed away for five fucking days? Arrogance. Stupidity. Just plain fuckin' ignorant.

Jack nodded as though he understood but he couldn't possibly. "But now you guys are older and you want each other. I can tell."

I laughed as we sat in my truck on our way to Dagger's place, where Jack would stay the night with Teddy. "Oh yeah, how?"

"Because you look at each other like this," he said and leaned forward, batting his eyelashes and looking away coyly before turning back with what I guess was supposed to be a smoldering look. "You both think I don't see it, but I do," he told me proudly, crossing his arms like a kid way older and wiser than ten.

Damn he didn't miss a beat. "Well your mom is a beautiful woman and I'd have to be blind not to notice."

"Yeah but it's not just that. Men always look at Mom but not the way you do."

I had no clue how to handle the fatherhood shit. My own dad didn't talk, not like Jack expected anyway. He'd only told me to wrap my dick up until I was ready to have a kid so I was way out of my depth with Jack and decided on brutal honesty. "I want Trina and I want you too, but I need to earn her trust again. I need to show her things can be different this time."

"But you're gonna do that, right?"

"Yeah kid, that's the plan." I ruffled his hair and he laughed.

"Okay. Good. I'll help if you want." Then he hopped from the car and grabbed his bag from the back, darting towards the door with me far behind.

"Hey Jack!" Teddy pulled open the door and they high fived before darting down the hall and leaving the door wide open.

I went inside to check in with Trudy. "Trina wanted me to let you know she'll take Teddy next week if it'll help."

She flashed a grin. "It always helps. How's fatherhood?"

"Jack is great. And I'm learning."

"And Trina?"

I raked a hand through my hair with a sheepish grin. "That will take a bit more time." But I was committed to trying, especially now that we had another night to ourselves. I stopped for beers and burgers, and even fucking flowers on the way home, because that's how I now thought of Trina's place. Hell, I didn't spend as much time here when Cherie lived here but now I couldn't seem to stay away.

But when I pulled up the only thing I could think of was murder at the sight of Wagman with his greasy fucking hair, leaning into a terrified looking Trina. I was out of the car in a flash, stalking up the walk and snatching a handful of the fucker's hair. My fist slammed into his face over and over and over, ignoring the blood that sprayed from his nose and mouth. The sickening crunch didn't faze me one bit, but the sound of Trina shouting my name loosened my hand and he fell to the ground and my foot kept him there. "Stay the fuck away or you'll end up joining your buddies. Soon." I kicked him several times in the stomach and once in the face. "Now get the fuck out! If I see you again Wag, I will fucking end you."

The asshole nodded and crawled across the lawn before pulling himself to his feet, flashing a sinister smile over his shoulder. "See you soon *Trina*."

"If you think that's true I hope your affairs are in order asshole!" Grabbing Trina around the waist I pulled her inside and kicked the door shut. "You okay Sweetness?"

She nodded quickly, too quickly, and those beautiful blue eyes were a tad too bright for my liking. "I am, actually. Thanks."

"You sure?" I cupped her cheeks so I could look deep into her eyes to see for myself. "If you're not say so. I'm right here babe."

Then that lush, kissable mouth spread into a sultry smile. "That was kind of hot, you know. And yes, big guy, I am completely ashamed that I think so."

Interesting. "You mean instead of flowers, beers and burgers I could have just kicked the shit out of someone to get you all wet and bothered?"

"Don't you mean hot and bothered?"

I shook my head and leaned in to brush a kiss on her lips. "Depends. If I slide my fingers inside you right now will I find you hot? Or wet?"

She shook her head. "Do I have a choice?" That husky laugh had my dick hard enough to pound nails. "Besides I do need to eat."

"Yeah me too," I told her and took her mouth, kissing her hard and fast, eating at her sweet mouth until she jumped up and wrapped those long sexy legs around my waist, urging me to do more. Her warm tongue and eager hips drove me crazy. "Trina."

"I want you Baz. Right here. Right now." She untangled her legs until her feet hit the floor, unfastening her pants and shoving them down along with a pair of sheer red panties. When she bent over the arm of the sofa, exposing that round, heart shaped ass to me, I lost all pretense of restraint.

I smacked her ass. "I missed this sweet ass," I told her as my cock nudged her opening and I sank in slow and deep. The sounds she made as my cock invaded her were low and strangled, incomprehensible and damn if my cock didn't harden at that. I plunged in and out, loving how much tighter she felt at this angle, hitting that spot that made her scream out. That flooded her pussy with moisture, coating me so I slid in easier. Faster. Deeper.

We came together hard and fast. Rough and necessary. Everything we both needed to forget about what the fuck had just happened. In no time at all Trina shook and convulsed, milking my cock. Her pussy sucked me in deep until every drop was wrung from me. A long minute later, Trina finally spoke.

"Now is the perfect time for beer and burgers." She groaned when I separated our bodies, pushing her ass back against me. "But I remember hearing something about flowers?"

Laughing at her playfulness I smacked her ass and lifted her in my arms. "First we shower." We both knew what that meant, another forty-five minutes—at least—before we were dry and ready for food.

And flowers.

"I'm starved, make it fast," she instructed.

"Hell no, this time we do it nice and slow. And wet."

She purred in my ear. "I know a little something about wet."

Fuck she was killing me.

Chapter Eight

Trina

Moving back to Brently was supposed to be a new beginning in a familiar place. It was not supposed to be a repeat of my past life, which included falling in love with Baz. Again. It's like I hadn't learned a goddamn thing as an entire decade passed. But the thing was, Baz was still a biker, still an outlaw, and I couldn't care less. He'd been a good father to Jack, a really great father actually, not to mention he'd taken on the role of protector for both of us. It wasn't smart and I knew it but the last time I tried to do what I thought was the right thing, the smart thing, it took me away from my home. Away from Baz. And eventually, right into the arms of the fucking psycho currently making my new life uncomfortable as hell.

Jensen had been my attempt at the steady, stable man with a good, reliable job. But he had one fatal flaw prior to the breakup and that was his indifference to

Jack. And then his inability to take 'no' for an answer had become a huge problem. Such a huge problem, it brought a madman to my doorstep. So, either I had shitty taste in men or I'd been using the wrong criteria by which to judge them.

Right now, I had to go with option B.

So this time, I decided to give my heart what *she* wanted, and that crazy bitch wanted Baz.

It was something I'd have to deal with later because I worked late last night and rose early this morning because we had errands to run. "Jack come on kiddo, we have to get out of here!" I knew he was still sleeping because the child was incapable of waking up before nine o'clock, so I closed the clasp on my earring as I walked down to his room, giving his door a loud knock. "Jack wake up or you'll be wearing pants that are too short for the next year!"

"Mom let's just do it online," he groaned, from what sounded like under his pillow.

I couldn't help but smile at that. "We have to try them on." Baz had gotten up early to help Mick move some things around for Talon so Jack and I were hitting some of the sales at the mall for all the clothes he continues to outgrow. Even though he hated shopping for anything but food, I knew he wanted to make a good impression at his new school next month. "If you think I'm running back and forth to the post office when your jeans don't fit, you better think again kid!" I heard a loud thud and then four distinctive steps before the door pulled open.

"Fine. I'll be ready in ten minutes." He flashed a sleepy smile then brushed past me into the bathroom.

While he showered, I slipped my shoes on and whipped up some egg and bacon sandwiches for us, honey wheat bread was my one concession to eating healthy this morning. I sipped my coffee and waited. And tried not to think about Baz. Or Jensen. Or the greasy asshole who kept darkening my doorstep.

"Breakfast sandwiches," Jack said as he slid onto a chair and chugged his orange juice.

"Yep. I figured they could hold us until lunch."

He nodded, chewing fast because he obviously had something to say. "Since we have to get jeans at the mall, Mom, can I get my t-shirts from this cool online store. Please?"

"Fine. Jeans, socks and underwear plus a couple of lightweight jackets today, t-shirts online. Please just be a good sport about it, okay?"

He smiled, looking so much like the little boy who used to climb in my lap and bestow hugs and kisses on me at will. I felt my heart squeeze. "I will. And thanks Mom, for bringing me here to meet my Dad. Love you," he said as he stood and pressed a bacony kiss to my cheek.

"You're welcome sweetheart. I'm glad he's everything you wanted in a father. And I'm sorry I waited so long to bring you two together." I figured I'd spend a few years making it up to him. "Get your sneakers on."

The kid never did anything slowly. He ran to his room and shoved his feet into his favorite pair of shoes before running back. "Ready. Can we have subs for lunch?"

"Sure." I pulled open the door and froze, standing in the doorway was a familiar head of perfectly coiffed russet brown hair and angry brown eyes that I once thought so appealing.

"Hello Trina. You are looking *mighty* fine this morning." Jensen raked a hand down my shoulder and I suppressed a shudder.

I took a step forward and pushed Jack behind me. "Run Jack!" The moment I heard the back-door smack shut, I pushed at Jensen's chest and stepped back to close the door.

"I don't think so Trina baby." He sneered and smacked his hand against the door, grabbing my hair and yanking me backwards until I cried out. "I've come a long way to get you, baby. How about a little kiss?"

As his mouth descended on mine, bile rose in my throat and I shook my head left and right, dodging his attempts to kiss me. He squeezed my jaw hard and when his mouth touched mine, I did the only thing I could think of, I bit down as hard as I could.

"You bitch!" He pulled harder on my hair until I bent backwards, trying not to puke with his angry glare filling my vision.

At least until his fist came flying right at my face, turning everything black.

Chapter Nine

Baz

"Okay babe, how 'bout that?" Mick spoke with the patience a man uses when his woman is pregnant, hormonal and maybe on the verge of a breakdown. But in fairness to him, we'd moved the big ass hutch at least five times already.

It was hot and I had sweat pouring from my body. I was more than ready to get back home to my own woman and child. "This is perfect for storage and you can use it as a sideboard for holidays," I told her just to end this torture.

She flashed a shy smile. "It looks great Baz, thanks. Both of you." She stood staring at the newly placed hutch, smile growing with every passing second. "Wash up and take a seat," she ordered as she disappeared into the kitchen.

"Thanks man. She's been a little eager about getting everything settled. Again."

"No worries. I'm happy to help."

"Good," Talon said as she returned with a tray of lemonade, brownies and sandwiches. "I appreciate it and I have another request."

"For me?" I couldn't imagine what she wanted me to do but Talon was good people so I'd do whatever she asked if I could.

"Yep. I want you to get Trina over here to sign my books."

My eyebrows went straight up. "You know what she writes? Let me see," I demanded a little too harsh but Talon only smiled.

"I do and I love them. Been reading them for a few years now. I'll show you," she said, stopping at the sound of her cell buzzing and ringing on the table. "Hey Trudy," she smiled but it quickly died and turned to worry and my body prepared for battle. "Hang on," she said and looked up, silver eyes bouncing between Mick and me. "Jack ran to Two Scoops, out of breath, crying and said his mom's ex showed up at the house. Go! Go! I'll be fine here. Go!"

"Call Darlington and let him know Jensen Murray is in town, violating parole," I told Mick and then I was out of my chair, through the front door and taking off on my bike in a matter of seconds. I headed straight home because I knew Mick and Dagger would check on Jack and keep him safe until I had this shit settled and Trina was safe. Cash texted with a description of this asshole and I pulled out my piece before heading inside.

I checked the front door. Locked. That was odd, so I decided to go in through the back just in case this motherfucker was still here. Though it might be more likely he'd try to take off with Trina. The back door was, thankfully, still unlocked which meant he hadn't checked the whole house. Inside nothing looked out of place which freaked me the fuck out with just how *not* out of place everything was. There were no signs of a struggle, not in the kitchen or the living room. Jack's room was typically messy but nothing more. Our bed, because that's how I thought of it now, was still made with her silky teal nightgown draped over the edge.

Her office door was closed, which wasn't all that unusual but one thing the military had drilled into me was trusting my instincts and right then, they told me that's where they were. I slowed my steps so they weren't as easy to follow, wrapping my fist around the knob and gun poised at the ready. I ducked as I pushed the door open and thank fuck I did because the bastard let off a shot.

"Go away asshole, she's mine!" His eyes were wild and wide. "Tell him Trina, tell that motherfucker you don't want him. You want me."

She winced at the way his arm tightened around her neck, the way the tip of his gun dug deeper into her head. He was a dead motherfucker as soon as I got my hands on him.

I flashed Trina a smile to show her I wasn't worried. Because I wasn't. This guy was a flashy corporate pussy, he didn't know shit about fighting or guns. I just had to bide my time. "How you doin'

Sweetness?" I made her the center of my focus so I could see and hear the truth.

"I'm o-o-okay Baz, just a little shaken up." She tried for a smile, but it was more of a frightened grimace. "Is Jack okay?"

I nodded, my gun still trained on Jensen. "Yep. My guys are looking out for him. He ran straight to Trudy and Dagger. Guess you didn't make it to the mall, huh?" Her smile angered that prick and he dug the gun into her temple.

"No more! Enough of this shit! Get out of here asshole, Trina is mine." His brown hair stood up on all ends, eyes wide and red. Crazed. The idiot was fucking high.

I grinned and stood taller. "Sorry to tell you dick breath but Trina here is mine. In fact, we're getting married and I'd really prefer not to splatter your blood all over my baby's office. But I will."

He barked out a laugh. "I hardly doubt that, grease monkey. Trina prefers a real man in a suit."

Jensen wasn't the first asshole to think that and he wouldn't be the last. But I had his number, so I leaned against the wall, legs crossed at the ankles so I looked calm. Unconcerned. "Aww Sweetness, you didn't tell him about me? That I was an expert fuckin' marksman? That I could hit him between the eyes before he even lined up a shot?" He paled and I couldn't help the shit eating grin that crossed my face. "Yeah I didn't think so."

He blinked as recognition finally dawned. "You're that little bastard's father? Good. Keep him and I'll take Trina, she belongs with me anyhow."

Bastard? My fingers itched to just drop this fucker where he stood for talking about my son that way but I knew I'd get my chance to lay a hurt on him before he left this room. "You're mistaken asshole, this is my family. I suggest you find one of your own or this won't end well for you. I guarantee it."

He laughed. "And what can you do, run me over with your motorcycle?"

"Actually, I plan to do much worse and only you can decide how bad it gets for you. See I'm the tech captain of my club but I got a guy who's a real expert hacker, trained by Big Brother himself to track down all that money you stole and your legit stacks too. He's already transferring it to untraceable accounts." I lined a shot up with a grin and he ducked behind Trina. Fucking coward. "What you stole will be returned and the rest well, let's just say it'll go to a very worthy club." I slid a look to Trina who still trembled with fear. "Still doing all right Sweetness?" She nodded and I gave her a wink. "Good girl."

"Shut the fuck up!"

I stood tall, shoulders squared and spoke as though he hadn't just thrown a little bitch fit. "So you can leave with your freedom, mostly in one piece and flat ass broke. Or you can leave in handcuffs, mostly in one piece and flat ass broke. What will it be Jensen? You have about oh…three seconds."

"You don't have the upper hand here, dick head!"

"Sweetness do you remember that weekend we spent in Vegas and those sexy shoes I wouldn't let you take off?"

She frowned but nodded, squeaking out a "Yes."

"Tick tock asshole." I kept my voice and my expression neutral and kept my gaze focused on Trina. "And remember that asshole who thought he could convince you to leave me and go with him?"

She smiled, warming up to the memory of us in Vegas, gambling, fucking and drinking. Not necessarily in that order. "You tried to step in, but I handled it." Her blue eyes flashed recognition and I knew she understood.

"That's right Sweetness." I winked and subtly tightened my grip on my gun. "So Jensen, have you decided on a bullet or a beat down? Personally, I'd go with the beat down because if you hurt Trina I will fucking shoot you where you stand."

His face was red with anger and his hand trembled. "You're wrong, grease monkey. I'll do what I want," he shouted and squeezed her neck tight enough to draw a cry of pain from her. "See?"

"You really shouldn't have done that," I told him, my blood boiling as my focus narrowed and I raised my arm, aiming the gun at him. Without blinking I squeezed the trigger and he cried out.

"Oww! Motherfucker, you shot my ear! I think I'm deaf," he shouted, clutching his ear.

"Now Trina!" She stomped his foot with all her might while he was distracted, causing him to drop the gun as she ran into my arms. "Good to see you, Sweetness," I grinned and wrapped my arm around her waist.

"You too," she answered breathlessly.

As happy as I was she was all right, I still felt amped up and in the mood for vengeance that this fucker had broken into our home and scared my woman and my son. "You want to come in my home and threaten my family?" I roared and grabbed that fucker by the shirt, rearing my fist back and let it loose right at his nose. "Scare my son?" My fist landed on his nose again, then his eye and his jaw. "You're lucky all I did was shoot your ear because if I wanted to, I could've shot you right between the eyes." I punched him once more because goddammit, he deserved it. "Think of it this way pretty boy, now your cellmate won't have anything to nibble on."

The bitch cowered on the floor. "Fine I'll leave. I didn't want the skanky whore anyway."

"Don't ever fucking talk about my woman like that," I growled and shoved the bottom of my boot in his mouth. "Got it?"

He nodded.

"I said, do you got it asshole?"

"Got it," he mumbled around my boot.

"Good." I removed my foot from his mouth and turned to Trina who watched warily like she didn't know what I'd do next but then, she grinned. "Hey Sweetness."

She walked into my arms as Sheriff Darlington entered the house with two of his deputies, guns drawn. "Everything all right in there?"

"In the office Sheriff. Everybody's alive."

"Well that's good to hear," he said sardonically as he stood in the doorway. "Wait outside," he instructed and I grabbed her in my arms and kept here there while we waited.

Fifteen minutes later we gave our statements and hopped in the car to go get our son.

Chapter Ten

Trina

Nearly a week had gone by since everything went down with Jensen, who was already back in a Connecticut prison cell, but things hadn't quite returned to normal. Jack still walked around jumpy as hell and scared all the time. He hardly left my side, deciding to forego the last two weeks of his classes at the community center to make sure nothing happened to me. He'd fall asleep each night in bed with me and Baz, which I knew Baz secretly loved.

He thought I didn't notice, but he smiled every time Jack's hand smacked his face in his sleep or snuggled close and yes, I found it wildly sexy how eager he was to experience all of parenthood. The good and the bad. He could've left the day the Sheriff carted Jensen to jail but he was in no hurry to leave and neither me nor Jack were in a rush to get rid of him.

I was, however, ready to move forward with him. Whatever that meant.

Done for the day, I pushed my chair back and grinned. My book was finally finished and ready to go to my editor which meant I had more than enough time to spend with Jack until he felt safe again.

I shut down my computer and closed the door behind me, changing into a brand-new sundress before joining my boys in the backyard. We had plenty to celebrate, starting with being alive and our new lives. Maybe a new whole family unit. And of course, the end of summer. I stood at the door and watched my two boys interact, they were both all smiles, green eyes shining with love and affection. And mischief.

"Look Dad, I got it!" At Jack's words, Baz bent forward to check out his latest skateboard trick.

"Pretty damn cool, kid." He beamed a proud smile that touched my heart and parts further south. Watching Baz be the dad I always wanted for my son was a huge turn on. And what it did for Jack, was a feeling I couldn't possibly describe. Each day Jack grew more confident and courageous. More outgoing and even though I hated it, more fearless.

I stepped out into the yard. "Hey guys, what's a girl gotta do to get some food around here?"

"You can start by kissing the chef," Baz told me as he beckoned me over, kissing me long and hard when I walked into his arms. I didn't know if it was the heat from the grill or the heat we always generated when we were together, but I felt hot and needy and downright sexy.

I pulled back, breathless and smiling. "I love the chef so kissing him is no hardship. Food or not."

His eyebrows wiggled suggestively and his arm tightened around my waist. "Good, because I have it on good authority the chef loves you back. In fact, I heard he plans to marry you."

I gasped at his words because the last I'd heard of it was while being held hostage by my crazy ass ex. "Oh really? Well just between you and me, Darlin', I can't wait until he asks."

He kissed me again, deeply and passionately and so filled with hunger I felt the first stirrings of arousal, quickly crushed by the sound of Jack gagging on the far side of the yard. "Good to know," he told me, emerald eyes shimmering with desire before he smacked my ass. "Go sit, the food's all done."

I glanced at the table, piled high with enough food to feed the whole club. "Are we having guests?" No one answered because they were too busy stacking their plates with food and eating. Like animals.

"Teddy is coming over later, but first we have some things to talk about," Jack said seriously. "I'd like to have dad's last name."

"Oh." I wasn't all that surprised so I nodded, chewing my burger slowly and waiting for whatever they had planned next. Baz took my hand and pressed a kiss to the inside of my wrist.

"Jack isn't the only one I want to give my name to, Trina. I love you, Sweetness. I have loved you since you drank me under the table that night you kissed me."

I had to laugh at that. "Oh I kissed *you*? You totally kissed me."

He shook his head, fighting the grin as Jack pretended to gag beside us. "Either way, it was the first of many great kisses. And more. And I want to spend the rest of our lives seeing what kind of kisses we'll share as we welcome more kids, get Jack his first motorcycle and of course, our honeymoon kisses."

"Ew, gross."

Baz laughed and reached over to ruffle our son's hair. "Sorry buddy but it's true. Your mom is a world class kisser."

Jack stood and stole a mini sausage from my plate. "I changed my mind about all this. If you guys are gonna kiss all the time, no thanks."

That drew a laugh from both of us as Baz turned his attention back to me and pulled out a small black velvet bag. He turned the bag upside down and dropped a ring in my hand. "Trina Mosley, I've never loved any other woman but you and ten years ago I fucked it all up. But this time, today, all I want is you and Jack. Be my wife Trina, let me make up for the past. Let us have the future we deserve."

My lower lip trembled as he plucked the ring from my palm and slid it over my ring finger. This was everything I wanted, ten years in the making. Now the chance was right in front of me, to have a life with the only man other than my son I ever truly loved and I nodded silently. "I can't wait to marry you Baz. So yes, I want all of that." Cupping his face, I kissed him, hard and fast. "But I don't need or want you to make up anything to me. Let's just enjoy now and make a great future for our family."

"Good because I have some ideas for future inspiration. Miss Chantilly."

I choked at his words. "How…oh my god! How did you find out?"

He rolled his eyes. "Jack and Talon dropped some pretty big hints but I am a tech god, you know?"

I laughed and wrapped my arms around him, feeling safe and content. Loved. For the first time in a very long time, I had that feeling of rightness, when everything in life just slides right into place. "Are you okay with this Jack?" I asked even though his beaming smile was answer enough.

He nodded. "Dad asked already and I told him yes. I get to be the best man."

"Then I guess we should start planning a wedding!"

Epilogue

Baz ~ One year Later

If anyone had told me last Spring that I'd be a father and a husband, I would've told them to quit smoking crack and get their head examined. But six months ago, on New Year's Day, I made Trina my wife and we now lived the perfect fucking suburban life. I drew the line at the white picket fence in front of our new home, but we had ten feet high wrought iron gates in case anyone thought they might want to go after my family.

Again.

Jensen would not only serve out the rest of his sentence, but he'd been tried and convicted of kidnapping, assault and stalking so he would serve more time in California after his sentence was finished in Connecticut. Wagman had apparently left town and we'd never have to worry about him coming back since he'd been found dead of an overdose at some shitty rundown hotel in Hollywood. Thank fucking goodness.

My family was whole. My club was whole. Life was fucking good right about now.

"Hey what's got that smug look on your face?" Trina pressed her sexy curves up against me, making my dick hard at the sight of her licking her lips.

"You Sweetness. Jack. Our life."

"Mmm, good answer." Puckering those soft lips and smashing them against mine, I wanted to take her right here on the deck of our new house, in front of all of our friends. And their kids. "Want something to eat?"

I shook my head. "I'm good. What about you Sweetness, want some meat?" I wrapped both arms around her waist, squeezing her ass when she pressed in close and let her fingers run through my hair.

"Don't I always?"

Yeah, my Sweetness was always ready to go. It was one of my favorite things about her, how hungry she always was for my cock. For me. Hell, as much as we went at it, I wouldn't be surprised if we added another ankle biter to the growing number of babies and toddlers now under CAOS protection. Talon had given birth to another baby, a little boy they called MJ while Kyla and Torch had another one brewin'. Their little boy Jason laughed nonstop as he chased Jack's new puppy, a blue-eyed Husky around the yard. Minx and Cash sat side by side, each holding a child with love shining in their eyes. "How about we slip back inside and I feed you a few inches?"

"A few?" She cocked an eyebrow and wore that sultry *come and get it* smile. "I'll take all nine thanks."

I groaned and kissed her behind her neck. "Let's go then." I pulled her inside and up the stairs to our new master bedroom and our big California king bed, perfect for all kinds of bedroom fun. "Damn I'll never get sick of seeing you laid out, so wet and dripping for me."

"You never have to, husband."

I grinned. "I'll never get sick of hearing you say that either."

On her knees, she crawled to the edge of the bed until we were face to face. "How about Daddy, do you like that one?"

"Fuck yeah," I told her, slowly undoing the buttons on her dress until her plump tits were exposed. Squeezing and kneading them, I savored the weight in my hand. "I love it."

"Do you think you'd want to hear it again?"

Was she saying what I thought she was? "Fuck Trina, all I want now is to put another baby in you, watching your belly swell and your tits grow."

She moaned when I pinched her nipples. "Good, I'm glad to hear it. Because I'm seven weeks pregnant."

I froze as her words sank in, then a smile split my face. "We're having another baby? For real?"

"Yep. I confirmed with the doctor yesterday."

"Aw baby that's the best damn news I've heard in a long time. I love you, Sweetness."

"I love you too, my outlaw husband. Forever."

"And then some." She laughed as I lowered her to the bed, kissing my way down her body.

"Better make it snappy so we can share our news while we have everyone here."

"Can't hurry greatness, baby."

Trina laughed, pushing at my chest until our positions were reversed. "Then I'll do it. Hang on Baz and prepare to have your world thoroughly fucking rocked."

I gripped her hips as she sank onto my cock, letting out that sexy little whimper that made me want to pound into her until my dick went numb. "You've already done that Sweetness. And then some." I don't know how in the hell I got so lucky but I made a promise to myself on our wedding day that I'd do everything I could to deserve this love. This happiness.

"In that case babe, just enjoy the view."

Damn straight.

* * * *

~ THE END ~

KB Winters

Acknowledgements

Thank you! I love you all and thank you for making my books a success!! I appreciate each and every one of you.

Thanks to all of my beta readers, street teamers, ARC readers and Facebook fans. Y'all are THE BEST!

And a huge very special thanks to my wonderful assistants and PA. Without you, I'd be a *hot mess! I'm still a hot mess, but without your keen sense of organization and skills, I'd be a burny fiery inferno of hot mess!! Thank you!

And a very special thanks to my editors (who sometimes have to work all through the night! *See HOT MESS above!) Thank you for making my words make sense.

Copyright © 2017 BookBoyfriends Publishing LLC

About The Author

KB Winters has an addiction to caffeine, tattoos and hard-bodied alpha males. The men in her books are very sexy, protective and sometimes bossy, her ladies are…well…*bossier*!

Living in sunny Southern California, the embarrassingly hopeless romantic writes every chance she gets!

Printed in Great Britain
by Amazon